PENNIES FROM HELL

Rosemary
>   an ingenuously beautiful model, had been had by the victim—in more ways than one.

Ball
>   the hardy American millionaire was eager for another killing.

Foskett
>   the thin, gray dealer held some curious secrets under his curious reserve.

Angela
>   ex-wife and actress, she played her toughest role for a little love—and a lot of money.

Fouad
>   the master silversmith boasted talents that put him way beyond the law.

One of them had marked Miles Cabral, and now his life wasn't worth a bent farthing.

It was left to Kate and Henry to find this strange fortune hunter—who had committed murder for a handful of coins.

D1570635

The Penny Murders

LIONEL BLACK

AVON
PUBLISHERS OF BARD, CAMELOT AND DISCUS BOOKS

AVON BOOKS
A division of
The Hearst Corporation
959 Eighth Avenue
New York, New York 10019

Copyright © 1979 by Lionel Black
Published by arrangement with Collins Publishers
Library of Congress Catalog Card Number: 79-56236
ISBN: 0-380-48090-5

First Avon Printing, February, 1980

AVON TRADEMARK REG. U.S. PAT. OFF. AND IN
OTHER COUNTRIES, MARCA REGISTRADA, HECHO EN
U.S.A.

Printed in the U.S.A.

CHAPTER 1

The auctioneer, up there on the rostrum, or whatever they call the pulpit-thing in an auction room, was making no attempt to work up the sense of excitement that Kate always associated with a great sale.

But this was a sale, she realized, for professionals. So, as aproned porters standing below the rostrum held up glazed tray after tray of coins, the auctioneer—rather come-on, really, the auctioneer, smooth young fellow, thick wavy brown hair, strong jaw, keen blue eyes, scarlet carnation in the buttonhole of his impeccable suit . . . What was she thinking? Oh yes, as tray followed tray, the auctioneer just murmured something about the coins, incomprehensible to Kate, and took the bidding *sotto voce,* mostly from the dealers in the first few rows.

The bids, admittedly, were astonishing.

"Ten thousand pounds, I have ten thousand pounds. Eleven. Eleven five. I have eleven thousand five hundred pounds. Twelve, thank you. Any more? Have you finished?" Tap. "Gone at twelve thousand pounds. Sleicher."

Kate tried to feel impressed. Twelve thousand smackers for a tray of old coins. Whew! But all she really felt was drowsy in this stuffy, dusty, sombre brown room. Numismatics was not, she thought, her thing.

But it was certainly Henry's. She glanced affectionately at her husband sitting beside her, his head tilting now and then appreciatively.

She nudged him. "Don't nod, darling. You'll get done for a tray of thalers if you don't sit still."

Henry turned and smiled gently at her. "No such luck."

It was because of Henry that she was here at all. She had gone across to the news desk and said, "Butch, there's this great coin collection coming up for auction. Hasn't been one like it for fifty years, Henry says. Like me to cover it?"

"What for?" Butch had asked, surprised. "The record bids will come in on the agency tapes. What else?"

"For Henry, really," she had admitted. "It's his hobby—in a small way, of course. He's got this coin cabinet he coos over. He says if I go with him, he'll steer me into a great story."

"Not a chance. But go if you want. I owe Henry for the drinks last Saturday. You might get a par out of it for the diary."

Even that, she thought, as she sat there patiently, now seemed improbable.

But there was rather more drama when a single coin was put up; a shifting of bottoms on these hard wooden seats, a murmur that might have been taken for excitement.

"A Charles I Oxford crown," Henry explained, awe in his whisper.

"That's something?"

"One put up at Glendinning's a few years ago fetched twenty thousand."

The bidding started at £10,000, and seemed to come from all over the place until it topped £18,000. Then she realized that it had become a duel. One contestant was a thin-faced, greyish man in the front row; the other an American—one of those tall, handsome, middle-aged, rather over-weight Americans—a few rows further back.

"Who are the two?" she whispered to Henry.

"The American's Cornelius Ball. One of the best-known collectors in the States. Fabulous. Comes from Chicago. Made his millions out of children's toys, then he was an ambassador a couple of times, somewhere in the Middle East. The fellow in the front row is a dealer, Harvey Foskett, very class, discreet rooms just off Bond Street. He won't be bidding for himself, of course."

"Then who for?"

"Could be anybody," murmured Henry, glancing round.

The bidding had reached £25,000. The American nodded his advance.

"I have twenty-six thousand, Mr. Foskett," said the auctioneer. Odd that he used his name, but this was an auction where they all knew each other. Rather like a family parlour game.

Kate saw the dealer slightly turn his head to the left, interrogative; then forward again. So his client was there.

"Twenty-seven."

"I have twenty-seven thousand pounds," said the auctioneer, looking at the American.

But Ball slowly shook his head, his face grim with annoyance.

"This superb specimen of the Charles I Oxford crown," intoned the auctioneer. "I have twenty-seven thousand pounds. Have you finished, gentlemen?"

Silence. Tap.

"Sold for twenty-seven thousand pounds. Foskett."

The next tray came up.

Henry nudged Kate. "I saw who Foskett was acting for. Might have guessed." He glanced to the left. "Miles Cabral."

Kate straightened. This was a news name. He had come up from nothing in the takeover games of the '60s, made his millions, and actually survived the crash in the '70s, when even Jim Slater fell on his fanny. Miles Cabral. Always in the shadows, never interviewed, rarely photographed. If she could get an interview with Miles Cabral . . .

"Which one?" she asked Henry.

"Second row, third from the left."

She picked him out, vaguely remembering an old news picture. In his forties now, middle height, thickset, swarthy. Said to be half Portuguese; a Portuguese name. Handsome. Was he a womanizer? Nobody knew even that, she thought.

"I didn't know he collected coins."

Henry nodded. "Reputed to have one of the finest collections in England. You try not to get that talked about—too risky. But numismatists know of it, of course. His is best known for a 'small change' collection—Athenian fractions of the obol, the first English pennies, rare United States dimes, that sort of thing."

"How did you recognize him, Henry?"

"My father acted for him, a few years ago, in a civil case that might have turned nasty, even a possible criminal edge to it. He's a tough, you know. Pa got the thing settled out of court. Cabral was grateful. I met him at dinner at home."

"Why did you say you might have guessed he was the other bidder?"

"Oh, he and Cornelius Ball are always at it. They're known enemies—as coin collectors, anyhow. Ball flies over from the States for every big London sale. Cabral is always there and they try to outdo each other. Usually Ball wins.

Today, Cabral's turn. You can see how pleased he's looking."

Cabral was glancing across at Ball with, Kate thought, not so much a pleased as a derisive look.

*

The auctioneer announced that he would resume at two-thirty and came down from his perch. Chairs were pushed back, people began to leave.

"I want to meet Miles Cabral, Henry."

Henry looked at her suspiciously. "Not like you to try for a newspaper interview that way."

"Of course not. Not unless I tell him, and he agrees. But it's a non-starter unless I meet him. How grateful was he to your father?"

"Well," said Henry doubtfully, "I'll try."

He pushed his way through the departing crowd, Kate close behind him, until he got to Cabral's elbow.

"Excuse me, Mr. Cabral. We have met. I'm Luke Theobald's son. You came to dinner."

The hard look on the man's face eased. He smiled.

"Of course. Your father is well? I'm glad. You're a lawyer too, I remember. What are you doing here?"

"I come to them all," said Henry. "It's my passion—not on your scale, of course."

"Really? Did you buy anything?"

Henry laughed. "At those prices? Out of my reach, I'm afraid. I saw it was you who got the Charles crown."

Cabral smiled again. "Was it that obvious? Foskett turning for orders after my limit was reached? I must tell him to be more discreet. Yes, I got it. A beauty."

"May I introduce my wife?"

"A pleasure," said Cabral.

The quick stare he gave her settled one question for Kate. Womanizer all right.

"What Henry dare not ask you, Mr. Cabral," she said, "is whether you would let him see your collection."

"Kate . . ." Henry protested.

But the man was in an affable mood. Kate had seen that.

"To show it to Mr. Theobald's son, and himself a collector, would be a pleasure."

"Oh, but sir . . ."

"Are you free for drinks this evening? You know where my house is? Just off Eaton Square."

"We'll find it," promised Kate.

"And you will come too, Mrs. Theobald? That increases the pleasure. Six o'clock? I shall look forward to seeing you."

He turned abruptly and was gone.

Henry said, "That was a bit of a fast one, Kate. You traded on the family, without telling him you're a newspaper reporter."

"No need to go into every little detail, Henry dear," she replied primly.

CHAPTER 2

The house stood in a blind alley, a double row of terrace houses, probably developed years ago from a mews. Cabral's addresses were not listed in any of the reference books, but the *Post*'s clippings library had them. His main home was in Sussex, on the South Downs near Brighton. This house in the cul-de-sac was his London pad. Henry parked the car on a meter round the corner.

The little street was ill lit, only a single lamp at the far end. Here and there were lights behind curtained windows, but Cabral's house showed only a glowing carriage lamp by the front door. It was the tallest house of the terrace; steps down a narrow, dark area to the basement, a Georgian front door, and two storeys above. A Rolls, presumably Cabral's, stood by the kerb. Its sidelights had not been switched off.

Henry rang the bell. Waited. No response. Kate said surely there must be a servant. Henry rang again, waited, then again. Nothing. There could be nobody in the house.

"But he said six o'clock," muttered Kate. "It's already ten minutes past." She held her wristwatch close to the nearside car lamp. "To be accurate, eight minutes past. And look, this must be his car."

Henry rang again. Waited. No response.

"The garage doors are open," said Kate, just noticing.

The garage occupied the ground floor of the house on the right of the front door. The basement area, she peered down to see, extended only under the left-hand side of the building. She moved towards the double doors of the garage, Henry nervously protesting that she should not.

It was blackness in the garage except for a faint penetration near the doors from the street lamp. Kate made out a switch on the wall, pressed it. The tube in the ceiling flickered, then shone brightly.

"Now look here, Kate, you simply must not . . ."

The garage was empty.

"It's odd," murmured Kate. "He asked us for six. His car's here." She giggled. "Perhaps he has run out of gin and popped round to the off-licence."

She stepped into the garage, Henry unhappily following. At the far end of the left-hand wall was a door that obviously led into the house. Kate tried the handle. It opened.

"Leave it, Kate."

"Maybe he has been taken ill," she said.

She stepped into the house. Henry came reluctantly as far as the door from the garage.

The entrance hall, oak panelled, graced with charming landscapes in thin frames, was softly lit. A sofa-table with the phone on it and a huge bowl of roses, a deep easy chair, an exquisite Persian rug, a moulded plaster ceiling. There was no sound.

Kate started towards the front end of the hall. Henry, standing ill at ease in the doorway from the garage, whispered loudly for her to come back.

There was only one room door, near the foot of the stairs . . . She hesitated whether to open it. As a test, she coughed loudly. Silence.

Suddenly she called, at the top of her voice, "Anybody around?"

It was startling in that silent house. There was no response.

Kate suddenly made up her mind, stepped to the door and opened it.

The room was brightly lit. She had an impression of bookshelves and little cabinets lining the walls, and a large red-leather-topped desk.

In that instant she also saw the figure sprawled on the floor by the desk, the pistol by the prone hand, the spreading stain of blood, the yellowish-grey little heap of brain substance on the richness of the carpet.

She recoiled, screaming. She was dimly aware of Henry running towards her.

Suddenly there was a loud knocking at the front door.

She dropped back into the easy chair, Henry gripping her shoulder.

"I'll be all right in a minute," she muttered.

The loud knocking came again. She saw Henry turn his head helplessly towards the front door.

Then there was a clatter from the rear end of the hall. Two police constables came running through the door from the garage.

For a few minutes Kate was still hazy from the shock. She could hear Henry explaining to one of the policemen that they had come to drinks with Mr. Cabral, got no reply, found the garage open, and so on. The other police-man was already on the phone, calling his station.

"Is that Mr. Cabral?" asked the constable of Henry.

Kate saw them move into the room, saw Henry's head nod. From her chair she could see the dead man's feet splayed on the carpet. The black leather shoes were new, looked expensive.

Suddenly there was another crash of knocking on the front door. One of the constables shouted, "Through the garage." The other made for the door to the garage, and a moment later returned, leading a sergeant, two more con-stables, and a short, rather stout, balding, middle-aged man in plain clothes. It was he who took over, stepped into the room, spoke quickly, authoritatively, to the constable, to Henry.

Kate's mind seemed now to come back into focus, so that she saw the scene clearly. The plain-clothes man re-turned into the hall, took the phone from the constable holding it, and gave a few sharp but quiet orders into it. Then he turned and came over to Kate.

"You've had a shock, madam. Are you feeling able to tell me about it?"

She nodded. "Yes. I'm all right now. It was a shock."

"Your husband says that, when you could get no answer at the door, you came in through the garage, thinking that, since his car was outside with the lights on, Mr. Cabral might have been taken ill."

She nodded again. "Is it Mr. Cabral in there?" she asked shakily.

"Your husband tells me so. We shall need further iden-tification, of course. So then you opened that room door. What did you see?"

"Just that," she said weakly. "He was lying on the floor. The blood, and the wound . . . the gun beside him on the carpet. I screamed, and Henry came running, and straight away there was that awful knocking on the door. I've never been so startled in my life. And then the police came running in, so quickly, it's incredible."

"Not really. This house is wired with an elaborate burglar alarm. When it is triggered off, it makes no noise in the house, but flashes a message by phone that comes up on the teleprinter in the Yard. That's the type of alarm we jump to. Get a patrol car here quickly enough and you trap the intruders."

"Us?" she asked faintly.

The detective slightly smiled. "There's no denying that you and your husband are here. What was the time when you came in through that door from the garage?"

"About ten past six. Just before I came in, I checked my watch by the car light, to make sure of the time. We were asked for six o'clock. It was then eight minutes past."

He picked up her wrist and compared her watch with his. "Not far out—a few seconds only. It was certainly you who set off the alarm by opening the door from the garage. The message to the police was timed at six-eleven and twenty seconds."

There were several more men bustling now from the garage into the hall—an obvious doctor with a medical bag, two plain-clothes policemen, a man with a camera. They all went through into the room. A constable who had been sent upstairs came down to report to the plain-clothes man: "Nobody else in the house, sir."

"You think he shot himself?" asked Kate, puzzled. "But he can't have done."

"Why not?"

"Surely a man who's going to commit suicide doesn't ask guests along to drinks."

The detective shrugged. "But it seems that he did."

"Couldn't somebody else . . . ?"

"This house has one of the most elaborate and effective burglar alarms in London. Nobody could get in or out without setting it off. And since the alarm message came when you opened the door from the garage, nobody could have left this house before you arrived, unless he possessed a set of keys to the alarm and could reset it after he had gone out."

"Then maybe . . ."

"Of course. But not very likely. Everybody who has keys must be known and identified. The only emergency set is held in safe custody elsewhere, and can be released only to us, the police."

He turned his head suddenly. The front door was opening. The man who stood in the doorway—a short, thin man, in a long black overcoat and broad-brimmed black hat, a muffler round his throat—was gazing in bewilderment.

The detective left Kate and stepped up to the newcomer. "I'm Detective Chief Inspector Comfort, from Scotland Yard. Who are you?"

"There's been a burglary?"

"Who are you?"

"Sorry, guv. Fred Sharp. I'm Mr. Cabral's manservant. What's going on, then?"

He had a London voice, not exactly Cockney, probably South-Bank suburban.

"You can identify Mr. Cabral, obviously," said Comfort.

"Identify? Something's happened to him?"

"I'm afraid so."

He led the little man into the room. Kate hesitantly followed; mercifully, somebody had covered the body with a sheet. Henry was standing over by the wall of cabinets, the police sergeant and one of the constables by his side. The room, she saw, had no window. It must have been blocked and plastered over. There was a small ventilation grille on the inside wall, near the ceiling.

The doctor was packing his bag, the photographer his camera. Another constable was carefully wrapping the pistol in a plastic cover. She turned her glance away as Comfort lifted the sheet from the figure's head, then dropped it back again.

The manservant was staring at the sheet. He looked dazed, shaken with horror.

"Somebody shot him?" he murmured. "Who shot him, then?"

Comfort gently shook his head. "There seems no doubt it was suicide."

Sharp stared at him. "Couldn't be. Not the guv'nor."

"You are familiar, of course, with the alarm system of the house. Could anyone get in or out without setting off the alarm?"

"Not a chance. Not without keys."

"Who has keys? Have you?"

"Not to the alarms. Only to the front door. Look, do you want to know how the thing works? Okay. There's two circuits. One's what they call the perimeter. You switches that on from a control panel in the coat cupboard in the hall. You can switch it on full, or part. When it's on full, it brings in every window and every door in the house, except the door to the coins room—that's this room—the door to the coats cupboard and the front door. Then you turns the lock in the front door—shunt lock, they calls it—and that brings in the front door and the coat-cupboard door."

"But not this coins-room door?"

"No. That's on the other circuit."

"You said the perimeter circuit could be switched on full or part. What happens when it's only part on?"

"That releases the kitchen door, on the landing at the top of the first stairs, and the doors and windows of the two bedrooms and bathrooms on the floor above. So when Mr. Cabral goes to bed, he switches the perimeter circuit part on, then locks the front door from the inside, and he can go upstairs to the bedrooms, and get anything from the kitchen if he wants. All the rest of the house is guarded."

"Except this coins room, eh?"

"That's on the valuables circuit. That's what they calls it. The control panel's in a safe in the wall just out there, in the hall, behind that picture of a windmill."

"How is that set?"

"Only Mr. Cabral can do that. The picture's hinged, like a little door. So he opens that, then opens the safe behind it . . ."

"With a key?"

"No. Combination lock. Only the guv'nor knew the combination. Then he switches on the panel in the safe, and that brings in a circuit of mats under the carpets, and photo-electric rays in front of the pictures in the sitting-room and the dining-room—same floor as the kitchen—and the silver cupboards, and specially here in the coins room. Then, when he's locking up, going out, say, or going to bed, Mr. Cabral locks this coins-room door. That's the shunt lock for the valuables circuit. It brings in the coins-room door, and the picture frame in front of the wall safe."

Comfort went over it again, ticking the items on his

fingers. "When the perimeter circuit is switched on full, nobody can open a door or a window anywhere in the house without triggering off the alarm to the police. When it's only part switched on, the door to the kitchen on the middle floor, and the doors and windows of the two bedrooms and bathrooms on the top floor can be opened without raising the alarm."

" 'Sright."

"When the valuables circuit is switched on, nobody can touch any of the pictures in the two rooms on the middle floor, or the cabinets in this coins room—in fact, can't get into this room at all. So the valuables circuit can't be operating now?"

"Not unless the phone's ringing like hell in Scotland Yard, guv."

"Which it isn't," said Comfort. "So Mr. Cabral must have switched off the valuables circuit when he came in. How about the perimeter circuit? Was that switched on full or part?"

"How the hell would I know, I only just got here. Go and look at the control panel in the coats cupboard. You can open the cupboard door now, because I unlocked the shunt in the front door."

"Constable," said Comfort, "have a look."

"Look, son," said Sharp to the constable, "there's a switch on the side of the panel. If it's pointing up, the circuit's only part on. Down, the circuit's full on."

The constable went out into the hall.

"Now then," said Comfort to Sharp, "the keys. How many sets are there?"

"Two. Mr. Cabral carries one. The other's the emergency set, in safe custody, that only the police can get hold of."

Comfort reached behind him and held out a small leather key-purse. "This was in Mr. Cabral's trousers pocket. Are all the keys there?"

Sharp took the purse and counted the keys. "Okay. All here."

"How about you? Didn't you need keys?"

"Only for the front door latch and the shunt lock. Like I told you."

"So you could have opened the shunt lock in the front door, got into the house and out again, locking the shunt lock behind you, within the past hour or two?"

"Could've done, guv. Except I was on the train up from

Brighton. The guard's an old mate of mine. He'll confirm it."

"We'll ask him," promised Comfort.

"Me and my missus lives downstairs in the basement when we're all in London," Sharp went on. "The basement ain't in the alarm system at all. Evenings, when Mr. Cabral's finished with me, I goes down the area steps outside. There ain't no indoor stairs to the basement, he got them taken out. When I'm gone, Mr. Cabral locks the circuits when he wants to go to bed. In the morning, I comes up the area steps and lets myself in through the front door. Then I goes up to the kitchen—the perimeter's always switched on part at night—makes Mr. Cabral's breakfast and takes it up to him in bed. Then I've got to wait in the kitchen until he's up and switches the circuits off before I can get into the rest of the house to clean up."

"Suppose there are guests."

"Then I takes their breakfast up too."

"Did Mr. Cabral sometimes have guests?"

"Times. Not often."

"Women?"

Kate saw Sharp hesitate. But then, "Sometimes."

"His wife?"

Sharp shook his head. "They was divorced, couple of years ago."

The constable returned from the hall. "The switch on the panel points downwards, sir."

"So the perimeter was full on," mused Comfort. "So nobody could have got out through the bedroom windows. Doesn't seem any possible reason to doubt that it was suicide."

Kate put in nervously, "Except he asked us to drinks."

The policemen turned towards her. "Have you known Mr. Cabral long?"

"Only today. We met at a coin auction this morning, and my husband, who's a keen collector, asked if he could see his collection. So Mr. Cabral asked us to drinks at six o'clock."

"Asked a couple of strangers?"

Henry said, "I knew him slightly, Chief Inspector. My father is a QC, who acted for Mr. Cabral some time ago, and I met him at dinner at my father's house."

"Your father is Mr. Luke Theobald, sir?"

Kate was amused at the deference which had come into Comfort's voice. Every policeman, of course, knew of the leading criminal lawyer of the day.

"That's right, Chief Inspector. As it happens, I'm a barrister too."

He handed over his card, which Comfort glanced at and put in his pocket.

"I'm not suggesting that this is a case of anything but suicide, sir. But, as a lawyer, you must realize that you and your wife coming into the house and setting off the alarm did call for explanation."

"Of course."

"Is it a very special collection of coins, sir?"

"Fabulous, they say. Especially what is known as Cabral's 'small change' collection—very rare coins of small de-nomination. Copper pennies shipped out to Maryland when America was still a colony, early United States half-dimes, Athenian fractions of the obol, and so on." Henry smiled. "None of that means much unless you are a coin col-lector."

"Worth a good deal?"

"Must be at least a quarter of a million, perhaps more. Only this morning we saw him pay twenty-seven thousand for a single coin, a Charles I Oxford crown, at auction."

"Could you check if it's here, sir?"

Henry smiled. "It may not have been delivered yet. The dealer who bid for him probably still has it. But I can look, of course, if that's all right."

When Comfort nodded, Henry turned to the coin cabi-nets, pulling out drawer after drawer, fascinated.

"I don't think the crown has been delivered yet," he said after a while. "The whole collection is beautifully arranged in matching sets, and sets in chronology. The Oxford crown would have gone, I think, into this drawer, but it's not there—only the space left for it."

"An empty space?"

"Nothing significant in that," Henry assured him. "A collector of Mr. Cabral's calibre plans the sets he will collect, prepares his cabinets for them, and leaves empty spaces which he fills as he gradually acquires the coins. For instance, look at this cabinet here. This holds the 'small change' collection I was telling you about. And it's the most marvellous collection I have ever seen. But look, there are empty spaces for the coins Mr. Cabral had not yet managed to get hold of. For instance, he has left room here for the 1794 American dollar, which very seldom comes on the market. Last time, about fifteen years ago, I think, a couple of them fetched around four thousand each at auction. They'd reach a much higher figure now. Then he has three eighteenth-century pennies, including a 1794 penny, which must be worth several thousand pounds." Henry smiled. "And he has left a few very optimistic spaces."

"Why optimistic, sir?"

"Well, here's a space for an Edward VIII twelve-sided threepenny piece—the only coin struck in that king's reign that did not have his father's portrait on it. The threepenny piece was never issued, but a few were struck and sent to coin-machine manufacturers to find out if the coin was practical. Undoubtedly some of them found their way into coin collections, and a few are known to be about, but very rare."

"Worth?"

"At a guess, a couple of thousand each." Henry chuckled. "And here are two spaces which even Mr. Cabral can never seriously have expected to fill—the 1933 and 1954 English pennies."

"Even rarer?"

"You probably know, Mr. Comfort, that the Mint produces each year only coins that are in current demand. If, for instance, there's a superabundance of pennies at any one time, they won't issue any pennies that year. That happened in both 1933 and 1954. In 1933 the Mint officially struck only six pennies, and they are all in museums or under foundation stones. But at least one more was struck unofficially, and the authorities are supposed to know where that one is. There could have been one or two more, who knows?

"As for the 1954 penny, officially there aren't any at all. A few were struck to test dies, but they were all supposed to have been melted down, with the dies. But, again, one was got out of the Mint somehow, nobody knows how. It was on offer several years ago by an American dealer for thirty thousand dollars. I don't think it is known who bought it—or if there is more than one 1954 penny in existence. It's possible. So perhaps Mr. Cabral was not entirely without hope."

"He didn't buy the one on offer in America?"

"Obviously not," said Henry, "or it would be here."

"Unless it were stolen," put in Kate diffidently. "Surely that could be a motive."

"Motive for what?" asked Comfort.

"Motive for almost anything," said Henry. "It would be worth much more than thirty thousand dollars these days—probably as many pounds."

"But not," said Comfort decisively, "a motive for suicide. There will have to be an inquest, of course, and you and your wife will have to appear. As a formality, too, I must have statements from you. This is Sergeant Chin. He will take your statements and get you to sign them. No need to go down to a police station."

"Do we have to do it in here?" asked Kate faintly, glancing at the floor.

"No, of course not. Chin, find somewhere for Mr. and Mrs. Theobald to give you their statements."

"Up in the dining-room," suggested Sharp.

"Very well," said Comfort. "And Mr. Sharp, I must ask you to stay until we have completed everything here, so that you can reset the burglar alarm. We must leave the house secure, of course. Will you be sleeping the night in the basement?" As a thought came to him, he added, "Is your wife there? Has she been in the building all the time?"

"She's not here. She's down at the guv'nor's house in Sussex, same as I was. Then I gets a phone call from Mr. Cabral this afternoon, telling me to come up to London, there was something he wanted me to do. Didn't say what. Yes, I'll lock up and set the perimeter alarm when you're through. Can't set the valuables alarm—don't know the combination for the wall safe. I'll stay the night in the basement."

The dining-room on the floor above to which the sergeant led the Theobalds was exquisitely furnished, and the paintings on the walls were, Kate guessed, almost priceless—certainly a couple of Picassos and a Cézanne, she thought, and two more she could not place.

The sergeant took out a notebook and asked Henry to begin.

"No need to trouble much about mine," Kate told him. "It'll be in the *Post* tomorrow morning in full, no detail omitted."

Sergeant Chin glanced at her sharply. "Are you Kate Theobald the journalist? And you're going to put it all in your newspaper?"

Kate smiled at him cheerfully. "I can't think of anything in the world that could stop me."

CHAPTER 3

Henry brought the dailies to the bedroom with the early morning tea. "You made the lead."

"So I should think," said Kate, gratified, sitting up in bed and reaching for the *Post*. It was spread across page one, shouting exclusive. The fact of Miles Cabral's suicide was not exclusive, of course. The Press Bureau at the Yard had put it out later that evening, so the crime men of all the dailies had it. What was exclusive was Kate's story, Kate's discovery of the body, Kate's detailed explanation of the best-locked house in London—locked electronically, unbreakably, with the keys in the corpse's trousers pocket. None of the others, she assessed as she scanned the rival front pages, had even got into the house, though a couple had blatantly lifted facts from her own story after the early editions came on the streets.

When she reached the office, Butch confirmed that none of the others had got in. The night desk, not knowing as yet of Kate's story, had rushed a couple of men along. But the house was silent and locked, Cabral's body had been moved to a hospital mortuary for the the autopsy. There was only the servant in the basement, Fred Sharp, who slammed his door and would say nothing.

"Nice work, Kate," Butch admitted. He was not addicted to praise. "Next time you feel like going on a cub reporter's assignment, just let me know."

"How about follow-ups?"

"There'll be some, of course. What happens to the great coin collection, what's in his will and all that. There'll probably be trouble over the will. He was divorced, as you know."

"Don't know the details."

"I got the clips from the library," said Butch, handing her the folder. "She cited him for adultery, but the case was undefended, so practically no court hearing, no juice."

"Angela Hughes," said Kate with interest, turning over the clips.

"Second-rate actress. She's on somewhere in London now."

"What do we know about her?"

"Not much," said Butch. "There hasn't been much to know. Since she left Cabral she's been shacking up with Mike Roseveare."

"I seem to know that name. Should I?"

"Young property developer, not much weight to him. Baronetcy in the family, but he won't get it, he's the younger brother. Like so many would-be property tycoons, he's thought to be in trouble."

"Maybe Angela will now be a rich woman."

"Maybe, and maybe not. Shouldn't think Cabral will have left her much, and a divorced wife doesn't have much status for challenging a will."

"Wonder who'll get it," said Kate. "There'll be a hell of a lot. Henry reckons the coins alone would fetch upwards of a quarter of a million."

"There'll be nothing said till probate is granted. But it might be worth ferreting round a bit." The phone light on his desk flickered. "It's for you, Kate."

"Front hall here, Mrs. Theobald. There's a man wants to see you. He won't give his business. He says you'll know. Mr. Fred Sharp."

"I'll come down," said Kate.

She took him to one of the small interview rooms. He was again wearing that too-long black overcoat, and holding the wide-brimmed black hat which he twiddled in his fingers as he sat facing her across the table. He looked worried, even a little distraught. His gaze kept flicking across to hers, then away again. When he started to speak, it was not much above a mutter.

"Read what you wrote in the paper, missus. But I don't think it was, couldn't have been. Not Mr. Cabral. So I thought I'd come and see you."

"Glad you did," said Kate. "Are you saying that you don't think it was suicide?"

"Couldn't have been. Not Mr. Cabral."

"But I don't see how it could have been anything else,"

argued Kate. "You yourself said that nobody could get in or out of the house without setting off the perimeter alarm if it were switched on full. And it was. I can vouch for that. I triggered it myself by opening the door from the garage. So it looks as though when Mr. Cabral came home he left the perimeter circuit switched on as protection while he switched off the valuables circuit and went into the coins room. Then the shooting. It was his own revolver. The Yard put that out through the Press Bureau. Where did he usually keep his revolver?"

"In a drawer in the desk in the coins room."

"Well, there you are. There could have been nobody with him, Mr. Sharp, because nobody could have got out before my husband and I came and started the alarm, and the police were there within minutes, and there was nobody else in the house. The only thing that still worries me a little is why Mr. Cabral left his car in the street with the lights on, when his garage doors were open and he could easily have driven in."

"Nothing in that, missus. When the guv'nor was driving the car himself, he always leaves it there. Then I comes out and puts it away."

"Then so what?" asked Kate, starting to feel irritated with the man.

"There was things going on," he said awkwardly. "I can't say about that. It was Mr. Cabral's business, and private. But there was things going on."

"You mean, suggesting some reason for somebody to kill him?"

The man nodded, twisting his hat. "Could be."

"Now look, Mr. Sharp," said Kate patiently, "whether or not there was somebody who wanted to shoot Mr. Cabral, he couldn't have done it in his house yesterday evening unless he had a key to the perimeter alarm shunt lock in the front door. Mr. Cabral had one of the only two sets of keys. The other was held by a key-holding company, to be surrendered only to the police if, say, the alarm went off accidentally. Directly I triggered the alarm last night, the police collected those duplicate keys. Mr. Comfort told my husband this. They were locked in the company's safe, and had never been taken from an individual strongbox since they were deposited there by Mr. Cabral, who signed his name across the seal. The only other possibility is that Mr. Cabral himself had a duplicate set cut to give to somebody else." She paused, thoughtful. "Of course, that is a possibility."

Sharp shook his head. "He wouldn't have done that, missus. He had them keys with him day and night, wherever he was. And that's easy proved, that he didn't get duplicates cut. They was registered keys. Even Mr. Cabral himself couldn't have got others cut without his signature to the lock company—and they'd have a record of that."

"I must mention that to Mr. Comfort," said Kate, "though I expect he has thought of it as a routine check. Must have done. So how can you possibly say it couldn't have been suicide? How could it possibly not have been?"

"Don't know how it was done, missus. But I'll take my oath it weren't that. Not Mr. Cabral, and with those things going on."

Kate said, "We don't seem to be getting anywhere, Mr. Sharp. Why have you come to see me? What do you expect me to do?"

"Look into it, missus."

Kate laughed shortly. "Look into what? You haven't given me the slightest thing I could look into, now have you, Mr. Sharp?"

The man sat in silence for a few moments, as though trying to make up his mind. At last he said, "There's this private detective the guv'nor was using, missus. He might know."

"Using for what? For his divorce?"

"No, it was after that. I don't know exactly what the guv'nor was using him for, but he'd know, the detective'd know, bound to."

"All right. Who is he?"

"Name of Grogan. I'd to meet him once, about something. He's got an office just off the Strand. He's in the phone book."

Sharp rose suddenly and made to leave. "Look him up, missus, this detective. Name of Grogan. In the book."

"All right, Mr. Sharp," Kate good-humoredly agreed, showing him back to the entrance hall. "If you say so, I'll look him up."

The private detective was in the phone book; an address in Henrietta Street. Kate took a bus up Fleet Street and got off in the Strand, turning up towards the Inigo Jones church, glowing warm, deep red even on this dull morning. She found the house, a notice board inside the door naming the small offices up to the roof. Arthur Grogan, Private Investigator, was at the very top. Patiently she climbed the stairs, brown linoleum wearing thin here and there, wondering why she was doing this, not expecting anything, not even with the feel of a hunch.

Arthur Grogan, Private Investigator, in worn black lettering on the clouded glass panel of the door, occupied the only office on the top floor. She had decided not to phone ahead, but just to call on the off-chance, so she tapped on the door. There was no response, so she opened it and went in.

She came at once against the stare of a very large, stout, solemn man with a walrus moustache, seated at a flat-topped desk on which rested the early edition of the evening paper, open at the racing page. The man neither moved nor said anything, but continued to regard her sombrely.

"Mr. Arthur Grogan?"

He acknowledged his name with a slow inclination of the head.

Kate took the chair opposite him at the desk. "I am Kate Theobald. I write for the *Daily Post*. You may have seen my report this morning of Miles Cabral's suicide. I am told he was a client of yours."

"That may," said Mr. Grogan—somehow Kate could not think of him as Arthur—"or may not be."

He was so wonderfully ponderous and the deep, slow voice so deliberate, measured. Kate knew as soon as she heard it that Mr. Grogan had once been in the Force. She could almost see him in the witness-box, slowly opening his notebook.

"I've come to see you," she said, "because Fred Sharp, Mr. Cabral's man, said I should—though I don't for the life of me know why. Fred Sharp is suspicious about something—I don't know what. He said I should come and ask you about the job you did for Mr. Cabral. So here I am," she concluded, feeling helpless.

"The enquiries I make for a client," replied Mr. Grogan gravely, "are of a confidential nature."

"Of course. But surely everything you investigate for any client is also of a confidential nature. Suppose I become your client, and ask you to report to me on the work for which Mr. Cabral engaged you. It can't matter to Mr. Cabral any more. What are your charges?"

"Thirty pounds per day, and proportionately for portions of a day," said Mr. Grogan, adding as an afterthought, "and expenses."

For no reason she could discern, Kate suddenly had a feeling that she was on to something. She took three £10 notes from her handbag and pushed them across the desk.

"I should like to be your client, Mr. Grogan. Suppose we regard this interview as a whole day's engagement—if you're free, that is."

Mr. Grogan stared at the notes for a considerable time. Then he reached a huge hand forward, picked them up and put them in a drawer in his desk.

His gaze returned to Kate. He methodically cleared his throat of phlegm, then told her, "Mr. Cabral engaged me to make a list of all employees of the Royal Mint who left that employment in 1954 or 1955, and to trace their whereabouts."

"How on earth could you do that, Mr. Grogan?" enquired Kate in an admiring voice.

"There are ways," he answered, ". . . and means."

He fell silent for so long that Kate wondered if that were all she was going to get. But then he went on.

"There were several on my list, but only three were still alive. I traced two of them with no trouble. It took me a month to find the third. He was living in a village in Devonshire, a retired person on a pension."

"Which village?"

"That is of no consequence, madam. The person in question has since deceased. It was what he told me that interested Mr. Cabral."

Long silence. After a while, Kate ventured to ask what the pensioned person had told him.

"He told me, madam, that he knew the man I was after, and he knew why. But that man was no longer living."

"Did you question him to make sure he knew why you were looking for that man?"

"No, madam. I myself did not know why. Mr. Cabral had not thought fit to inform me of the purpose of the investigation. But when I reported the outcome of my enquiries to Mr. Cabral, he seemed assured that I had traced the man he wanted to know of. He sent me back to Devonshire, to enquire whether there were any close relatives still living of the man the pensioned person had referred to."

After a long silence, Kate asked, "And were there?"

"There was a niece, madam, the man's sister's child. But the person I interviewed could not recall the sister's married name, and therefore did not know the niece's last name. Her first name, he told me, was Rosemary. He also told me that Rosemary was a handsome young person, and well developed. He made some jokes on that score, madam. When he last met her, he said, she was working in London as a photographic model for fashion magazines and advertisements and such. He did not know her whereabouts, but said he thought she could be traced through a photographer for fashion magazines and advertisements and such, by name of Simon."

"Simon what?"

"Exactly what I asked him, madam. He said Simon nothing. Just Simon. I apprehended that this must be the photographer's trade name."

"And did you trace Rosemary through Simon?"

Mr. Grogan slowly and significantly shook his head. "I was prepared to do so. But when I reported the result of my further enquiries to Mr. Cabral, he said that that was all the information he required, and that was the termination of my engagement."

"And there is nothing more to tell?"

"Nothing more, madam."

"Mr. Grogan," said Kate, rising, and trying not to look at the newspaper racing-page on the desk, "this has been a useful enquiry for me. I feel, moreover, that I have probably kept you away from some other most important investigation, and that I ought to make a further payment in respect of, shall we say, expenses. Would five pounds be adequate?"

She put the note on the desk.

Mr. Grogan inclined his head judiciously.

"That, madam," he conceded, as the huge hand advanced once more over the desk, "should cover it."

Kate was still chuckling when she got back to the office.

"Take me off the news diary for a few days, Butch," she requested. "I'm trying a sort of follow-up to Cabral."

"What's it about?"

"I don't really know yet. It may be about nothing, a complete nonsense. But I'd like to look a bit further into it. I'll tell you if anything hardens."

She walked across to the corner of the big room where the women's-page editress sat, at the only desk with a vase of flowers on it, and a rug beneath the feet.

"Tell me, Jean, is there a fashion photographer named just Simon?"

"Sure. He's an old queen with a studio somewhere in Notting Hill." She opened her contacts book and scribbled on a piece of paper. "Here's his address and phone number, if you want him. He used to be near the top, but he's a bit past it now. I used him quite a lot years ago. He's a dear old thing. The girls still like working for him. They know they're safe. I did hear he runs a discreet sideline in male-model soft porn. Is that your angle?"

"No, no. Just trying to find somebody he may know. Thanks a lot, Jean."

Kate's taxi turned off Notting Hill Gate and made its way up the Portobello Road, then threaded west. The house was on the fringe of the black area; once a fine Regency or early-Victorian house, now shabby. The arrow of a handwritten sign pointed across the small front garden, past the withered skeletons of michaelmas daisies and goldenrod, and a couple of rose-bushes still thinly budding, and down a few stone steps to the basement studio.

"I've come to see Simon," she told the thin young man in T-shirt, jeans and plimsolls who answered her ring.

"He uses only his regular girls."

"Thanks for the compliment. But I'm not a model. I'm from the *Daily Post*. Kate Theobald."

The young man grinned and beckoned her in.

"Newspaper, eh? He'll love that."

The two basement rooms had been opened into one to make the studio. There were floodlights suspended from the ceiling and on floor-tripods; movable spots here and there. It must once have been a rather charming little studio, but the lavender paint of the walls had faded and the flats stacked to one side were worn round the edges, patched in places.

On a bench near the glass door that led out to an ill-tended rear garden sat a couple of girls in loose wrappers, one sucking at a Coke bottle through a straw. In the studio centre, against a pale grey flat, a really beautiful girl in a nightdress open well below her breasts was posing on a gilt wickerwork chair. A short, tubby, elderly man was circling her with a Rollei, calling to her to turn her head this way or that, or show a little more of those delicious thighs, sweetheart, and don't be shy.

"Hey, Simon," called the young man who had brought Kate in.

"Oh Roger, do shut up, dear. Can't you see I'm busy? It's crucial."

"There's a newspaper reporter to see you."

The photographer turned round, startled, delighted. He came towards Kate, dropping his camera on the strap, hands extended.

"Kate Theobald," she said, "from the *Daily Post*."

"My dear, dear young lady. What a pleasure. You want an interview?"

"Sort of. Is there anywhere we can talk?"

"My office, darling." He waved to the model. "Take a rest, Lulu. And you others. Roger, get them some coffee, there's a sweetie."

The office was in a back addition to the house. On the way, Kate saw that what had been the kitchen beyond was converted into a darkroom. The office itself was a small room with a one-bar electric heater struggling to cope with the chill. The walls were pasted all over with photographic prints, mostly of girls, but a few of near-naked, muscular young men. The French escritoire was piled high with letters, bills, envelopes, more prints. There was room for only two fragile-looking chairs, to one of which Simon waved her.

"And now, my dear young lady—or should I say young person?—what can I tell you. For the women's page, I take it."

"No. I'm looking for someone."

"Looking for someone? Oh." His disappointment was so childish that Kate had to suppress a smile.

"I am trying to find a girl named Rosemary, and I'm told she modelled for you."

"Ah yes, she did. But not any more. A few months ago someone else came to ask me to help find Rosemary. A gentleman. I put him into touch with her, and not long afterwards she ceased to model for me. One of the other girls told me he had set her up in a flat in Kensington." He sighed at the wickedness of the world. "Yet he seemed a gentleman of civilized taste. And Rosemary is such a silly girl. Pretty, I grant you, in a kind of simpering way, but quite empty-headed. No thoughts, no conversation." He sighed again. "Some men are very stupid about sex."

"Can you help me to find her?"

"But why, dear lady? Why?"

"I think she might be able to clear up a small point in an enquiry I am making."

Simon shrugged. "Lulu may know."

He went to the door and called her. The girl in the nightdress came in, a shawl round her shoulders. But even so, thought Kate, she must be damned cold.

"Lulu, this lady wishes to get into touch with Rosemary Ward."

"Because of Mr. Cabral?" asked Lulu.

Kate nodded.

"Dear me, how sharp you are," murmured Simon, "how acute. It had not occurred to me. I had forgotten his name. Mr. Cabral. So . . ."

"Why do you want to find her?" asked Lulu suspiciously.

"I think she could do herself quite a lot of good," said Kate. "Miles Cabral was very wealthy. His wife divorced him. There will be a great deal of money lying about. Simon tells me Cabral set her up in a flat in Kensington."

That seemed convincing to Lulu. She opened up a little. "He did for a few weeks. Then he threw her out."

"But she has not returned to me," protested Simon plaintively. "I could use her, as ever. Figures like hers are rare; nauseatingly exaggerated, perhaps, but uncommon."

"She went back to her former boy-friend. He was Mr. Cabral's excuse for ditching her. Mind you, she was a bit stupid about it, not very discreet. Asked the boy-friend to a party given by Mr. Cabral at her flat. Then they got high and there were ructions. So now she's living with her boy-friend. He got her a job in a theatre—in the box office, or the bar, or usherette or something. He's a young actor."

"What's his name?" asked Kate.

"Jonathan Parr."

"Know where he lives?"

Lulu shrugged. "Haven't a clue. Somewhere Streatham way, I think, or maybe Clapham. Somewhere ghastly, anyhow. I say, come on Simon, let's get this bloody picture done, eh? I'm freezing."

Kate made her apologies and they returned to the studio, the thin young man, Roger, being called to show her out.

As he opened the front door, Roger grinned. "You looking for a girl-friend? Don't count on Lulu. She's definitely hetero—hetero-nympho you could say. She even tried it on me. Me!"

Kate said nothing, but turned and walked quickly up the steps to the little front garden.

"Ta-ta," Roger called after her, mocking.

CHAPTER 4

It was Kate's day to lunch with Henry at his club; they met there once a week, in the ladies annexe of course, through a side entrance. But after all, Henry pointed out, they did allow women in the dining-room. Several of the older members had resigned when that decision was reached by the committee.

Kate, looking at the bill of fare, declared she would make it a fish day—smoked salmon, then a sole. Should it be *Véronique* with white grapes, or *à la Dugléré*, cooked in white wine with tomatoes and shallots? *Véronique,* she decided. Henry grunted and ordered onion soup and steak-and-kidney pudding. A half-bottle of Chablis for the lady and a demi-carafe of club claret for himself.

"What I must tell you, darling," she said as the meal began, "is what happened this morning. First of all, Mr. Fred Sharp called on me at the office."

"Fred Sharp? Oh yes, Cabral's manservant. What the devil did he want?"

She told him—of Sharp, then of Mr. Grogan, then of Simon.

"Not that I've the slightest idea what it all means, but I'm beginning to feel there may be something."

Henry was gazing at her thoughtfully. "It could mean something quite extraordinary. A 1954 penny."

"I'm not with you."

"Don't you remember my telling Comfort last night? In 1954 there were no pennies issued. The Mint had made the dies, but then it was decided there were too many pennies in circulation and none would be needed that year. A few had been cast, to test the dies, but those coins and the dies were all supposed to have been melted down. However, it is known that one was kept and somehow smuggled out of the Mint, because it was on sale in America a few years ago. If one, why not two?"

"So Cabral . . . you mean he was on to it?"

"For years there has been a sort of whisper among numismatists that a second 1954 penny was in existence. Suppose Cabral decided to find out. He hired the comic detective to get him a list of Mint employees who left that year or the next. It was a long shot, of course. Even if somebody had smuggled out a second penny, he need not necessarily have given up his job. But if some of his colleagues suspected, it would perhaps be safer to leave. That's how Cabral must have reasoned."

"Could he have been right?" asked Kate.

"Well, there was that fellow-worker, the pensioner in Devon, who told Grogan that he knew the man he was looking for, and why. That would suggest that he knew there was a smuggler, and what he had smuggled. But the smuggler himself was dead. The only contact was a niece, Rosemary, working for a fashion photographer in London, your friend Simon."

"So Cabral used Simon to get into touch with Rosemary and got her into bed with him," said Kate, following the train of argument. "Set her up in a Kensington flat—isn't that a lovely Edwardian period touch?—in the hope of discovering what had happened to the 1954 penny uncle had snitched."

"But didn't find it," Henry pointed out. "It was not in his coin cabinet—just the empty place waiting for it."

"So when Cabral failed to get it, he threw Rosemary out. It fits, you know."

The waiter arrived with the main dishes, the wine waiter with the wine. So they dropped the talking; first things first, as Kate always felt about a pleasant meal. But when they had both sat back contented, refused a sweet or cheese, and were sipping coffee, she returned to the penny theory.

"I reckon it's worth going on a bit further, Henry, don't you?"

"As a pure matter of numismatics, indeed I do. But you won't get a newspaper story out of it. Cabral didn't get the penny. Maybe it doesn't exist. He committed suicide—not for that reason, of course."

"I wonder why he did," mused Kate.

"Heaven knows. Maybe it'll come out at the inquest. There could be all sorts of reasons—business disasters, a woman, mental breakdown, lots of possibilities."

"Henry, I'm going to get in touch with Rosemary. I rang the Spotlight casting directory and got Jonathan Parr's address. That's the young actor she's living with. It is in fact in Clapham, just south of the common. Can you make a few enquiries among your numismatic friends about the rumour of a second 1954 penny—what strength there is to it?"

"I suppose I could try Foskett," he said doubtfully.

"Who's he?"

"A dealer. You saw him at the auction. He was the one acting for Cabral in the bidding for the Charles I crown, remember?"

"Oh yes. Do you know him?"

"I've bought a couple of minor things from him, and Father used to deal with him quite extensively a few years ago. My father has a very creditable coin collection. It's what first aroused my interest."

"Okay, Henry, you do that," she said, getting up. "Thanks for the lunch. It was delicious. Now I expect you're retreating to the sacred part of your club to have a nice masculine glass of port or something. I'll creep out the tradesmen's entrance. See you tonight."

It was only a short walk from the club to Foskett's rooms in Albemarle Street. Nothing so vulgar as a shop. Merely the name, Harvey Foskett, on a small walnut plaque beside an inconspicuous doorway; on the floor above, an ante-room where a severe-looking, bespectacled girl sat at her desk, and a charmingly furnished reception room beyond. A few choice coins under glass in Adam-style display tables; most of the treasure, as Henry knew from a previous visit, in a massive safe hidden in a wall cupboard.

When Henry was shown in, Harvey Foskett laid aside the magnifying-glass through which he was studying a coin on the leather top of his elegant desk, and said, "Ah, the *young* Mr. Theobald."

"Not my father, I'm afraid," replied Henry cheerfully. "The young and impoverished Mr. Theobald."

"Equally welcome," said Foskett, coming round to offer Henry a deep armchair, seating himself in another beside him. The chief impression of the man was grey—grey hair, grey formal suit, long thin sallow face. When he smiled, it was as though he was forcing his lips to shape themselves; no smile anywhere else in that face.

He was smiling now, as he asked, "How can I be of service?"

"I find myself in need of a little extra cash, Mr. Foskett. I am thinking of selling one of my coins. What would you say to a 1738 two-guinea piece?"

"I would ask how long you have possessed it," replied Foskett cautiously.

"About six years. It was a birthday present from my father."

"Then it is probably all right," Foskett assented. "I should have to examine it, of course. But if it is a genuine piece with, say, a VF rating . . . let me see, it has double R rarity, but that has been somewhat debased by the counterfeits in existence. Somewhere between six and seven hundred?"

"I'd hoped for rather more. I shall have to think about it, Mr. Foskett. Are there so many counterfeits?"

"Of that particular coin, yes. It was one of the Chalhoub basics. You know about Chalhoub? Oh well, he is a counterfeiter who works in Beirut—or did. I have not heard of him recently, and hope he was not involved in the Lebanese slaughters. He is one of the finest coin technicians there has ever been, outside government Mints. His work was perfectly legal. In Lebanon, as in several other countries, it is no offence to produce counterfeits of coins that are not in current circulation. Had they been passed in Lebanon, possibly an offence would have been committed, but they were not. An American named Harry Stock took them elsewhere and disposed of them singly from batches of twenty."

"Isn't he the chap who was caught in Switzerland a few years ago?"

"That's the man. But he had had about a five-year run for his money—or rather, for his counterfeit money," said Foskett with another mask-like smile. "He disposed of quite a number of those two-guinea pieces, and Chalhoub's technical ability was so remarkable that they are extremely difficult to detect. There have been counterfeiters throughout history, of course, some of them famous—Samuel Casey, Christodolous, Wyllys Betts and so on. But none ever produced such remarkable copies as Chalhoub. Some of his counterfeits were of exactly the same density as the original coins, and even when the alloys he used were slightly below standard, it was rarely by more than a tiny fraction."

"Astonishing."

After a pause, Foskett said, "I read your wife's account in the *Daily Post* of the Cabral tragedy. Poor fellow. He had so much—and yet to kill himself. What an unhappy coincidence that you chanced to be there. It must have been a ghastly experience, especially for Mrs. Theobald."

"It upset her, certainly."

"And it simply arose, as she reported, that you met Mr. Cabral at that sale, and he invited you to drinks, to see his collection?"

"Just that. In fact, I had met him once before, and my father had acted for him professionally. What do you think will happen to his collection, Mr. Foskett?"

"If it comes on the market, it will be sensational. As a dealer, I know some of the treasures which he acquired over the years, and doubtless there are others I am not aware of."

"There's a rumour," said Henry, "that he even had a 1954 penny. Could that be possible?"

Again that forbidding smile. "The famous 1954 penny story! There is one in existence, as you know, because it was offered for sale by an American dealer. But I have a shrewd idea of who acquired that, and it was not Miles Cabral. For many years the story has been going round that there was a second penny smuggled out of the Mint. I suppose it could be true. But I have never heard of any real evidence to support it. So I simply do not know, Mr. Theobald. If it does exist, then I suppose it is equally possible that Miles Cabral had covertly bought it."

Henry shook his head. "He hadn't. I looked at the 'small change' collection during that dreadful hour in his house last night. There were several unfilled gaps waiting for the coins to be acquired, the Edward VIII threepenny piece, the 1933 penny and the 1954 penny among them."

"You looked at the coins?" asked Foskett, seeming surprised, almost shocked.

"The Chief Inspector asked me to," Henry explained. "Since he knew I was interested in coins, because that was the purpose of our visit, he asked me if Mr. Cabral had a really valuable collection. I assured him he had collected some of the most expensive coins in existence, and in-

stanced the Charles I crown that you had bought for him
that morning. So he asked me if it was there. It wasn't, of
course. I told him you could scarcely have delivered it so
quickly."

Foskett's face was now bereft of any smile.

"It was not for Mr. Cabral that I bid for that crown."

"Oh, come on, Mr. Foskett. That's just professional caution. I saw you glance at Cabral to get sanction for that
last bid. And, in fact, when we met him, he admitted the
purchase was for him."

"I should be obliged, Mr. Theobald, if you did not
repeat that. I bid for the crown for a client, of course.
His identity is my affair. I am certainly not admitting that
it was Miles Cabral. I have had to pay for that coin.
Would you really expect me to wait for my money until his
will is granted probate, and his executor starts to admin-
ister his estate, probably months ahead, possibly years?
Twenty-seven thousand pounds, Mr. Theobald, not including my commission. So let me assure you categorically that
my client is not Mr. Cabral. As a lawyer, you will no doubt
appreciate at once how damaging it would be for me if
that story got about."

Henry took the warning good-humouredly. "Understood,
Mr. Foskett. You can rely on me, and I'll tell my wife."

Foskett rose. "That would be prudent, sir. And you'll let
me see your two-guinea piece if you decide to sell?"

"Of course," said Henry, rising to leave, shaking Foskett's outstretched hand. It was a long, bony hand, cold to
the touch. He really was, Henry thought to himself,
amused, an absolutely typical art dealer.

It had started to rain as Kate picked up a taxi to take her
to Clapham. As they crossed Albert Bridge in its bright-
painted gaiety, the afternoon was closing in and the river
misting over. Shops lighting up in Battersea Park Road and
Lavender Hill did not much enliven the dreariness of the
mean streets between. There were electric flares in the middle of Clapham Common, where little groups of men were
struggling in the rain to put up the big tops for the annual
circus; already the sleek motor-caravans were lining the
Avenue.

The address she had for Jonathan Parr was in Alfriston
Road, a block away from the south-west side of the common. He would be in digs, of course; not an expensive dis-

trict, and handy for an actor, only a few minutes' ride by Underground from Clapham South to Piccadilly.

A middle-aged woman in overall and cardigan answered Kate's ring at the door of a heavy, red-brick Victorian house.

"Mr. and Mrs. Parr?" she enquired tactfully.

"Top floor front."

So it would be just a bed-sitter, Kate reflected as she climbed the stairs through a lingering smell of boiled cabbage from somebody's lunch. Her knock on the door of the top floor front was answered by a man's "Come in."

He was lounging across the rumpled double bed, reading a paperback novel by the light of a small table lamp; an attractive young man in heavy sweater and jeans, longish blond hair, good features, sensitive.

"I'm looking for Rosemary," she said.

"She's shopping something for tea. Back soon. Friend of hers?"

"No. I'm from the *Post*. Reporter. My name's Theobald."

The young man raised himself. "Kate Theobald?"

Kate glowed. "It's pleasant to be known."

"I suppose it's about Miles Cabral. Glad the bastard shot himself. But I don't think Rosemary can help you much. He threw her off weeks ago. But wait, by all means. I think I can hear her coming upstairs now."

The girl who came in, pulling the scarf from her head and trying to shake off the rain, was quite remarkably pretty; dark hair flowing in waves down her back, big blue eyes, pert nose, slim figure and really magnificent breasts, swelling, firm, the nipples outlined through the damp blouse above her jeans.

"Got caught in the shower," she said. "Damn. I'm soaked. Hallo. Who are you?"

Kate plunged. "I'm Kate Theobald, from the *Post*. I want to talk to you about Miles Cabral."

The girl giggled. "Does all the world know I was sleeping with him?"

She put down on the wooden table the shopping basket she was carrying.

"I heard it from Simon, and a girl in his studio, Lulu."

"You get around."

"I do my job."

Jonathan Parr, unpacking the shopping basket, said, "I'd ask you to tea, but it's kippers, and we've got only two."

"I'd like to stay—just a cup of tea. I couldn't eat anything. I had a big lunch."

"Okay," he said, switching on a Baby Belling electric cooker on a table by the window, shoving the pair of kippers on to the grill while the girl flicked a cloth over the table, set out the crockery, sliced a brown loaf, extracted a quarter-pound of butter and a pot of strawberry jam from a cupboard that served as larder and wardrobe. The smell of the kippers grilling was strong but not unpleasant. Jonathan was lifting the electric kettle, brewing strong tea in a brown earthenware pot.

"We have to eat now," he explained. "The rest of the evening we're at the theatre, and it's too much of a bloody nuisance to cook supper when we get back. Also, by then, we want to go to bed together."

"Johnny!" the girl protested.

But she smiled at Kate.

When they were settled round the table, the girl asked, "What can you possibly want to know about Miles now? He's dead, and that's that. Oh, I forgot. You were the one who discovered him. Did he look . . . well, messed up much?"

"Not too good."

Rosemary bit at her lip. "I'm sorry. Oh, I know you loathed him, Johnny. But he wasn't a bad chap. He was very kind to me—at first, anyhow."

"Where did you meet him?" asked Kate.

"Simon gave a party, and Miles was there. I've never known Simon give such a party before. Champagne flowed —the real stuff."

"I expect Miles paid for it."

"Why should he? To meet me? Oh, that's silly."

"Anyhow, he did meet you, and asked you to dinner next evening, I suppose, or something like that, and called to pick you up in his Rolls."

Rosemary giggled. "Something like that."

"How long before he started talking to you about coins?"

Rosemary stared. "How do you know he did?"

"I guessed. He did, didn't he?"

The girl nodded. "After I'd been in the flat a couple of weeks or so, he asked me to dinner at his house. It's a marvellous house—oh, but of course, you've been there.

Sorry. Anyway, after dinner he showed me his coin collection." She giggled again. "Didn't mean a thing to me. But I told him, joking, that I had a collection too. It was my uncle's. Uncle knew about coins. He used to work in the Mint. Then he was killed in a car accident. I was the nearest relative—my mum and dad are both dead—so I got what he left. It wasn't much. Some National Savings certificates and a couple of hundred quid in a building society, and the coins. Uncle lived on his pension, but that stopped."

"Miles said he'd like to see your collection?"

"I'd got it in the flat in Kensington. It wasn't very big—just a wooden cabinet with drawers that pulled out, that you could stand on a sideboard or something. I had it in a cupboard."

"So Miles said he would sell it for you?"

"I don't know why I have to tell you," said Rosemary, "if you know it already."

"I'm still just guessing. Did it fetch much?"

"About fifty pounds. Why are you asking me all this?"

Jonathan cut in. "I'll tell you why. Kate thinks that there were some really valuable coins in the collection, and he kept them and sold the junk. Isn't that why?"

"I'm certainly wondering," admitted Kate. "Were there any pennies in your uncle's collection, Rosemary?"

"Haven't a clue. I never studied the coins. Just a few old coins they were to me."

"Didn't I tell you, Rosie?" demanded Jonathan. "Wasn't I right to challenge the swine? I should have insisted."

"You challenged Cabral?" asked Kate.

"I asked Johnny to a party at my flat in Kensington," said Rosemary. "Miles was there, of course. Then Johnny got tight, and shouted at Miles that he'd cheated me out of some valuable coins. Miles told him not to be silly. So Johnny said he must produce a list of the coins he had sold. He said he demanded a list. So Miles got angry, and asked what the hell it had to do with him. And Johnny said he was speaking up for me, because I was his girl, and maybe we'd get married. Not that we have." She grimaced at him. "Not sure that I like him enough. Anyway, the row at the party got worse and worse, and Johnny tried to hit Miles, and Miles walked out, and next day he sent a message to me to get out of the flat."

"And you did?"

"Of course she did," said Jonathan. "I insisted."

"What I don't understand," pondered Kate, "is why he didn't simply give you a list. He could have left out any coins he'd taken."

"But we have Uncle's list," Jonathan told her. "He didn't know that, but he must have suspected when I asked for a list of what he had sold."

"Could I see it?" Kate asked Rosemary.

"Sure. It's Uncle's old notebook. I'd forgotten I had it until Johnny reminded me, after I'd given Miles the collection to sell."

From the top drawer in a chest by the wall she took a worn black-leather notebook. Kate looked through it. There were jottings about various coins the old man had been after, notes in a small, crabbed but clear hand-writing, on certain rare coins, one or two newspaper clippings pasted in. Some of the notes were sprinkled with a sort of numismatic shorthand—RR, FDC, R^3, Unc. Towards the end of the notebook was Uncle's own list. She ran her eye down it, careful not to show surprise.

"Well?" asked Jonathan.

"I don't know anything about coins myself," said Kate. "But my husband does. He's a keen collector. May I borrow this list to show him? I'll return it, of course. He will be able to give you a fairly sound estimate of what the collection was worth. I think it must be quite a lot more than fifty pounds."

"You see?" cried Jonathan triumphantly to Rosemary. "I was right."

When Henry got home that evening to their little walk-up flat in Chelsea, Kate had the drinks out ready for him. He mixed her a gin and vermouth, and poured himself a scotch.

"I need that," he said. "When I got back to chambers there was a brief for me. I've had my nose stuck into it for a couple of hours."

"Good one?"

"Looks promising."

"How about Foskett? Did you get anything out of him?"

"Nothing much, except a warning not to go round saying he bought that Charles I crown for Cabral. I can see his point. If he admitted that, he'd have to wait for the estate to be settled before he got his money. So, of course, he will sell it to somebody else, possibly for more. Anyway, he'll collect his commission."

"Anything about the 1954 penny?"

"Only confirmation that there has always been a rumour of a second specimen, and an assurance that Cabral was not the owner of the one that was sold in the States. What's the model girl like?"

"Humdinger to look at but, as Simon said, not all that bright. You were right about Miles Cabral's motive for seeking her out and getting her into bed—though that alone wouldn't be much of a hardship. Uncle had a coin collection, which passed to Rosemary when Uncle was killed in a car smash. Cabral showed her his coins room, and of course she then recalled Uncle's coins, which she had forgotten all about. Cabral offered to sell them for her, and later gave her about fifty pounds, which he said were the proceeds.

"Rosemary, the dear little noodle, was delighted. But Jonathan wasn't. He got himself invited to a party at the Kensington flat, quite deliberately, I'm sure, to pick a quarrel with Cabral. Rosemary was his girl-friend before all this happened, and he hated Cabral for snatching her. So he worked up a furious row, and in the end was trying to hit him."

"The row was about the girl, of course."

"No. About Uncle's coins. Jonathan loudly accused Cabral of cheating, saying he kept the valuable coins for himself and sold the rest. Cabral denied it. Then Jonathan demanded a list of what had been sold. Cabral never produced one. Next day he flung Rosemary out."

"Why couldn't he simply have come up with a phoney list?"

"Presumably, because he wondered if the youngsters might have a check-list. And they have." She handed him the notebook. "Take a look at Uncle's list in the last few pages."

As he read it, Henry put down his whisky and straightened in astonishment.

"It's fantastic. A 1933 penny, an Edward VIII three-penny, and a 1954 penny. If he really had them . . . You say he worked at the Mint? Those are the three really valuable rare coins that could have been brought out surreptitiously. Heaven knows what they'd fetch in the market."

"And the rest?"

"Nothing much. Just an ordinary amateur's collection. But those three . . ."

"I went back to the office," said Kate, "got this note-book photocopied so that I could return it to Rosemary, and then I wrote a Cabral follow-up story. Oh, I was very, very careful. I wrote that there was a rumour among numismatists that Cabral had in his collection a 1954 penny. I explained about the penny. Very romantic I made it. Then I worked in a bit about his wife having divorced him, and speculation as to what would happen to this great coin collection, and all his other wealth, when his will was read. I hinted that, whatever he had willed, it might be challenged by several women who might claim to have been his common-law wife—pure hokum on my part, of course, but it made a lovely story. The only thing I didn't put in was the fact that the 1954 penny had disappeared from his coin collection."

"How do you mean, disappeared?"

"If Uncle's list is right—and why shouldn't it be?—then Cabral had taken those three special coins before he sold the rest. They weren't in his 'small change' collection, because you looked last evening and those spaces were empty."

"But my dear Kate, that doesn't prove anything. It could well be, as I said, that they were simply blank spaces left for coins he wanted to acquire."

"And had acquired. Surely that notebook is evidence enough. He had the coins—and they weren't there when you looked."

"But that implies . . ." protested Henry.

"Of course it does."

"But how about the locked house, the burglar alarm?"

"I don't know how it was done, Henry. But now I'm beginning to think that Miles Cabral did not shoot himself. And I'm going to hunt around until I find something strong enough to let me say so on page one of the *Post*."

CHAPTER 5

The woman on the telephone was speaking English with a heavy foreign accent.

"Is that Kate Theobald, please? I must tell you an important thing. Your article in the newspaper this morning about Mr. Cabral and rare coins . . ."

Not a European accent, Kate thought. Not the thickness of Africa, nor the sing-song of India. Somewhere in Asia maybe, or the Middle East.

"Yes? Something about my report this morning?"

"Stop, Miss Theobald. Do not go on with that. It is dangerous for you."

One of the usual mentally-upset people who telephone newspapers.

"Who are you?" Kate asked. "What is your name, please, and your address?"

"My name is nothing to you, and I not tell you my address. Only I warn you. Stop, or it will be dangerous for you."

"Dangerous in what way?"

"If you go on, something will happen to you."

"Oh, come now," said Kate good-humouredly. "This is an English newspaper. Nobody decides what does or does not go into it except the editor. Certainly no outsider."

"I am not telephoning for you. I am telephoning because there is somebody who might be tempted . . ."

Her voice tailed off. There was a long pause.

"Tempted to do what?" asked Kate at last.

The answer was suddenly the telephone pips. So the caller was in a call-box. Perhaps she would put another 2p in the slot and resume. Kate waited. But there was nothing more. She replaced the receiver, thinking little of it. Just one of the oddnesses that the telephone arouses in some people—heavy breathers, mouthers of obscenities, angry people trying to reach a Minister, or a member of the Royal family, or a famous sportsman, or a newspaper writer. Pitiful.

She returned to reading the photocopy of Uncle's note-book. A boy had been despatched to Clapham to return the original to Rosemary.

Butch came over. "Anything more on Cabral?"

"Not yet, Butch."

"You want to stay with it?"

"For a few days. It might develop into quite something."

"All right," Butch conceded. "But it'll have to be a bit firmer than your piece this morning. Think-pieces are okay on a features page, but I'm not keen on them in the news columns. Yours this morning was a bit thin on facts."

"I couldn't write what I suspect, Butch. And I'm not going to tell you, either. Nothing like hard enough yet. But if it turns out as I think it may, you'll see that this morning's piece is part of the build-up."

She reached for her phone, which was pulsing.

"Is that Miss Theobald? It's about your report in the *Post* this morning."

No doubt of the accent this time; standard American.

"Speaking."

"I was very interested, Miss Theobald, in what you wrote. My name is Cornelius Ball. I'm something of a coin collector myself."

"My husband has spoken of you, Mr. Ball. He says you're one of the leading numismatists in the States."

"So? Well, it's pleasant to be flattered. Your husband is interested in numismatics?"

"Infatuated."

"Say, that's fine. I suppose I made an error in addressing you as Miss Theobald, not knowing you are a married lady."

"Not to worry, Mr. Ball. But in fact, Mrs. Theobald."

"It's this English 1954 penny, Mrs. Theobald. I'd be mighty interested to learn anything more you may know about it. Why don't you have lunch with me? I frequently take lunch at your Connaught Hotel. You know it?"

"Of course."

"If you're free for lunch today, Mrs. Theobald . . . I have to return to New York tonight."

"I'd be delighted, Mr. Ball."

"I'll be looking for you, ma'am. About one o'clock."

As she hung up, Kate said to Butch, "There could possibly be a more factual story there."

"What about?"

"Don't know yet. But at least I get lunch at the Connaught. Some of the best food in London, Henry says. Not that he has ever taken me there. Too bloody expensive, he says, to waste on a wife."

*

Feeling thoroughly contented with life, Kate sat in the charming little entrance drawing-room to the Connaught, waiting for Cornelius Ball. He had sent a message, the hall porter told her, apologizing for having been delayed. He would be there very shortly. No, Mr. Ball was not staying at the hotel. He had a London flat near by. But of course they knew him very well at the hotel.

He came through the revolving door, glanced at the porter's desk for guidance, then crossed the room towards her. He was even more handsome than she had seen across the dimness of the auction room. He had an open, kindly face and an evidently powerful frame—tall, broad shoulders, long arms and legs. He walked briskly, athletically.

Perhaps he was a little older than she had guessed; probably nearing fifty. His suit was beautifully cut and yet somehow, indefinably, not English. The cost of a bespoke suit, Henry had complained the other day, was getting prohibitive, but his tailor had assured him that in New York it would cost at least double. But, of course, Cornelius Ball was a millionaire.

He greeted her with outstretched hands, sat beside her and beckoned a waiter, ordering two dry martinis, American strength, with olives.

"One place in London you can get a decent martini," he assured her cheerfully. "But that's one of the very few things I hold against your city. I love London."

He talked pleasantly of his many visits here, the wonderful times he had had, the charming people he had met. The drinks arrived. Delicious, Kate told him. Stimulating. Cornelius Ball laughed happily and pulled out a silk handkerchief to dab at his well-trimmed blond moustache.

Kate wondered when he was going to touch on the reason for his invitation, the *Post* story that morning. But nothing was said until they were seated in the dining-room and he had ordered lunch with an expertise that would have impressed even Henry. He must, she thought, have been a wonderful ambassador.

At last he came to it. Had Kate any reason to suppose that Miles Cabral had owned a 1954 penny? "There is one in existence. It was offered for sale by an American dealer —but of course you wrote of that. When it was offered, I happened to be on safari in Kenya and did not hear of it until it was too late. It had been sold. I never did find out who bought it. Since you wrote of it this morning in connection with Miles's suicide, I wondered if you had discovered that it was he."

"If I had, I would have said so in my piece this morning."

"Then why . . . ?" he asked, slightly puzzled.

"Something to keep the interest up, Mr. Ball. As I sometimes say to Butch—he's the news editor, what you would call the city editor—what do you want, a good story or an argument?"

Cornelius Ball smiled. "Just speculation, then, without any foundation? So why pick on that particular coin?"

"Because Mr. Cabral was trying to collect it. He had left a space for it in his 'small change' collection. But there was no coin there."

"You examined his collection?" asked Ball, surprised.

"Not I, but my husband. It's because Henry's so interested in coins, and is himself a collector, that Mr. Cabral asked us there that evening."

"Your husband is a newspaperman?"

"No, a barrister—a lawyer. It runs in the family. His father is one of the leading advocates in the London courts. And, incidentally, also a keen numismatist. He had once acted for Mr. Cabral, which is how Henry knew him. So when Henry explained to the Scotland Yard man the reason for our being there, the Chief Inspector asked him to take a look into Mr. Cabral's cabinets, to see whether the coin he had bought at auction that morning was there. In fact it wasn't. But Henry had a good look at some of the collection. The coin from the auction simply hadn't yet arrived. By the way, Henry happened yesterday to meet the dealer who was bidding at the auction—bidding against you," she added mischievously. But Ball only nodded gravely.

"He still has that coin," she went on. "And he insists he wasn't bidding on behalf of Mr. Cabral. The reason, as

Henry pointed out to me, is that the dealer certainly isn't going to wait for his money until the Cabral estate is settled up. So, if you still want that coin, maybe you could now get it."

"I have already made an offer for it, my dear young lady, at rather less than the price it fetched at auction. That price was at least twenty per cent too high, simply because Miles and I were bidding against each other, and we have long been—er—rivals."

"I hope you get it," said Kate. "Anyway, that was the basis for my piece this morning—the Scotland Yard man's asking Henry to take a look. Henry was rather impressed with him. Chief Inspector Comfort, his name is. He looks very ordinary and plain, but Henry reckons he's one of the best men at the Yard. That's what Henry's father told him, anyway."

Ball nodded. "A keen brain behind that rather dull façade."

"You know him?"

"I met him when I went along to Scotland Yard, to tell them that I had called at Miles's house that afternoon."

Kate almost gaped. "You were there?"

"We had a chat after the auction, and Miles asked me to come along for drinks. He said he had some people coming in—you and your husband, evidently. I took a taxi and was there at about five-thirty. That's the hour Americans start the evening's drinking." He smiled. "I forgot that you British hold off until six. I rang at the door for a while but got no answer. So I said the hell with it and came away."

"You mean," asked Kate, "that Mr. Cabral hadn't got home yet?"

"I think he was there. His Rolls was outside, with the sidelights on. I don't know why he didn't answer to my ringing, unless . . . But that's not a very pleasant surmise. Anyway, I thought I'd better tell your police and ask if they wanted me to stay for the inquest. Inspector Comfort said it wouldn't be necessary. All he required from me was a sworn statement. I was glad of that, because I need to fly back to New York tonight. I have some heavy business dates. The Inspector said the inquest would be straight-forward anyway, the verdict would be suicide, and there was nothing useful that I could testify in person."

"What I can't understand," said Kate, "is why a man who is going to shoot himself asks people in for drinks."

Ball raised his hands in perplexity. "Who can fathom the workings of another man's mind when he has reached that point? But the fact is there. Shoot himself he did, and I think I know why."

"You do?"

"I can guess. There were aspects to Miles Cabral . . ."

"Aspects?"

Ball glanced at her sharply, then slowly shook his head. "The man is dead. So leave it at that. But I don't think there will be many bitter tears shed."

For a moment such malevolence had shown in his eyes that Kate was startled. But then he was his suave, smooth self again. It was as though, she thought, a match had suddenly flared and illumined a hidden face, then snuffed out. Now come on, girl, she told herself, don't start imagining nonsense. But she could not avoid wondering whether Miles Cabral and Cornelius Ball had been rivals, not only as numismatists, but as men.

The waiter arrived with coffee. Ball looked at his watch and said, "I shall have to ask you to excuse me if I leave you soon. I have some business documents to read, and my packing to do, and I always try to reach Heathrow a little early. It can be chaos."

"Sure."

"By the way, how did you find out about Miles's women?" he asked, sipping his coffee.

"What women? Oh, you mean my piece about his divorce, and maybe there were other women who might contest the will. We have a clippings library, of course, and a record of the divorce was there. She divorced him for adultery, but as the case was not contested, there was little reported."

"She had ample grounds," said Ball softly, "ample grounds."

"You knew about it?" asked Kate, interested.

"I knew Angela well. She and my sister were close friends. They were at Oxford together as students. Whenever Angela came to the States, she stayed with us. Ursula, my sister, who was unmarried—as I am—kept house for me in Washington. It was through Angela that I first met Miles Cabral, when Ursula and I made a stay in London some years ago. And then . . . But the story is of little interest." He saw Kate's look of dissent. "And, for me, too painful."

"I'm sorry," said Kate awkwardly, but not understanding.

Cornelius Ball turned on his frank smile. "But that was not what I meant, Mrs. Theobald. The fact that Miles was divorced is, of course, public knowledge. But you wrote of other women who might contest his will."

"What do you want, Mr. Ball," asked Kate demurely, "a good story or an argument?"

He laughed. But the laugh seemed a bit forced.

"I can see that you thoroughly deserve your reputation as a great newspaperwoman."

Over supper in their flat that evening Kate kept on putting the question to Henry: "Why did he ask me? I don't get it. What did he want?"

"To know whether Miles Cabral had a 1954 penny?"

"I don't think it was that. He didn't seem particularly interested. Anyway, he would know when Cabral's collection comes on the market, as I suppose it must once the will has been granted probate."

"To let you know that he had been at the house that afternoon?" Henry wondered. "But why should he want to do that? He had already been sensible enough to tell the police, in case they wanted him for the inquest. And what did it matter anyhow? He didn't get into the house."

"We have only his word for that."

"Not so. We have the burglar alarm. Even if Cabral had let him in, and Ball had shot him—which seems to be what your fevered imagination is suggesting—he couldn't have got out again without triggering the alarm. And we know it wasn't triggered."

"Then it must have been the women," Kate decided.

"The women? Oh, you mean that question about who were the women you'd invented who might challenge the will. What could he possibly want to know about them?"

"I don't know," Kate admitted. "What I do know, or at any rate feel fairly sure of, is that Miles Cabral had those special coins he had filched from Rosemary—and they weren't in his cabinet when you looked. So what happened to them?"

"There could be a dozen reasonable explanations," Henry protested. "All you're saying is pure speculation. But there is one certain and known fact. Nobody could have shot Cabral and taken the coins out of that house without alerting the police. And the police were not alerted until you blundered in."

CHAPTER 6

The inquest was held at Westminster coroner's court in Horseferry Road. It was a bleak, wintry morning. Kate and Henry took a taxi from Chelsea along the Embankment. The river was high, a string of barges surging against the flowing tide, a little police launch sneaking upstream in the shelter of the far bank.

The coroner was late and by the time he took his high seat the courtroom was full. Kate hoped the hearing would not go on too long in the smell of wet mackintoshes and sweat.

For the first half-hour there was little to interest her. The police evidence was simply an account of what had happened that evening, and confirmation that the bullet which caused the death had been fired from Cabral's own weapon, which was found on the floor beside his body. The only amusing moment was the revelation that the Chief Inspector's true name was Aloysius Comfort. When she and Henry had been giving their statements, the sergeant had referred to him as Bill.

The coroner gave the gist of Comfort's evidence when he had finished. "You are implying, Chief Inspector, that until Mr. and Mrs. Theobald arrived there could have been nobody in the house except the deceased, because of the elaborate system of burglar alarms?"

"That is so, sir, unless somebody had a duplicate set of keys to the perimeter alarm circuit and the front door. This has been fully investigated, and the police are fully satisfied that the only duplicate keys in existence were held in a strongbox by the most reliable keyholding company in London, to be produced only to Mr. Cabral or the police —and were produced to the police directly Mr. Cabral's death was known. The manservant, Mr. Frederick Sharp, has keys to the two locks on the front door, but we have confirmed that, at the relevant time, he was travelling by train from Brighton to London, and the keys were in his possession. Mr. Cabral's own keys were in the pocket of the trousers he was wearing."

Medical evidence followed. Death had been caused by a gunshot through the right temple. Details. Yes—in answer to the coroner—the angle of fire and the skin-scorching around the wound were consistent with the revolver having been held in the deceased's right hand when the shot was fired.

Then came Frederick Sharp, to go all through the explanation of the burglar alarms again, and to give the coroner the same assurances. Without his long black overcoat one could see how very thin Fred Sharp was. Such a short, skinny man, not much bigger than a young boy. He looked uneasy, Kate thought, when the coroner asked him if he had any reason to think that Mr. Cabral might take his own life.

"No, sir. Not the guv'nor. Not Mr. Cabral."

"You speak as though you were devoted to your employer."

"Always very good to me, the guv'nor," Sharp mumbled.

As he came back to his seat in the courtroom he glanced anxiously at Kate. At least that was the impression she got. Anxious.

It was Henry's turn to enter the box and relate what had happened that evening. The coroner did not keep him long and did not question him at all about the coin collection. It was clear, Kate understood, that the coroner was already satisfied that it was suicide. The circumstances were not important. The only outstanding question was why a man of Miles Cabral's wealth and status had killed himself.

The evidence required of Kate was even briefer. She was happy about that. She had no intention of saying anything that might arouse the curiosity of the reporters crowded at the Press table, most of whom she knew well. The slightest hint would set three or four of them digging.

When the coroner dismissed her, merely condoling for the shock she must have suffered, she smiled as sadly as she could and resumed her seat. With any luck there was no news story of consequence in this inquest.

Then it came.

The coroner recalled Chief Inspector Comfort to validate a statement by Mr. Cornelius Ball that he had called at the house that afternoon and had been unable to get any response at the door, though the deceased's car stood parked outside with its sidelights lit.

Comfort confirmed that the statement had been made, signed and witnessed in his presence. "Mr. Ball is an American citizen, sir, and he had urgent matters requiring his attention in New York. He came voluntarily to Scotland Yard. Since his evidence related only to the time when the deceased was probably already in his house, it seemed to me that a sworn affidavit would be sufficient."

"Quite sufficient, Chief Inspector. But the other persons who volunteered information to you have, I believe, more to tell us."

"That is so, sir."

The coroner nodded to his officer, who called the next witness. "Miss Angela Hughes."

Kate straightened in her seat, startled. She could see the heads round the Press table lift in sudden expectation.

The woman who went up to the witness stand had been seated at the back of the court and nobody had noticed her.

Kate stared at her; Cabral's ex-wife. She was quietly dressed, nothing flamboyant at all, nothing of the theatre. She wore a beige woollen suit and a plain felt hat. A blonde, but fading. She must be well into her thirties, Kate guessed. Her face was a little drawn; perhaps only the strain of this hearing. Good features, large blue eyes, a figure starting to fill in anticipation of middle age, but still reasonably neat. Lovely hands, long fingers, graceful. When she spoke, her voice was quiet, low-pitched with an attractive huskiness, and the words clear.

She gave her name and occupation, actress. Yes, she had been married to the deceased but the marriage ended in divorce two years ago. She had seen very little of him since. But on the day on which he was to kill himself she had telephoned him at his club at lunch-time, asking to meet him. To discuss certain business matters, she told the coroner. Miles had invited them to come to his London house at four o'clock.

"Somebody was to accompany you, Miss Hughes?"

"George Roseveare, a friend who has been advising me

on certain business matters in which I was still involved with my former husband."

"Mr. Roseveare is your accountant?"

Her head tilted slightly up and she spoke with even greater clarity. "No. We are living together. We intend to marry when George's divorce is through. And that is nobody's business but ours."

Kate saw the coroner's face slightly harden. He remained immensely courteous, but evidently intended to have nobody dictating to him in his own courtroom.

"Business in which the deceased was involved very shortly before his death is relevant to this enquiry, Miss Hughes."

"It concerned a company that Miles had set up in Guernsey some five years ago, and of which he had made me a director. We were then still married, of course. I took no part in the operation of the business and did not try to understand it. I had, in fact, forgotten all about it until I was served last month with some papers concerning it."

"Served?"

"By a firm of solicitors. George thought this was monstrous and said we must insist that Miles should release me from any involvement in the company. That was what we went to see him about."

"What papers were served on you?"

"Something to do with a debt the company owed. I don't really understand it. Miles said it was of no importance, some clerk's mistake. He said he hadn't been aware of the debt and he would have it paid off at once. George said that wasn't the point. Miles must not only release me from the board of his Guernsey company, but must give me a written undertaking that would absolve me from anything that had occurred in the past. Miles said he'd arrange that."

She's lying, Kate suddenly thought to herself. That woman is lying. Kate had no idea why, or what it was all about. She could not have given any reason for supposing that the woman was lying. She just suddenly felt certain that she was.

"This discussion took place in Mr. Cabral's house that afternoon?" the coroner was asking.

"Yes. George and I got there at four o'clock. At first there was no answer at the door. The house was obviously empty. I was furious. I thought Miles was just fobbing me off and wouldn't turn up. But George said give him a chance, he might have got held up somewhere. So we sat in the car and waited. And about ten minutes later Miles drove up and let us into the house."

"Was the burglar alarm in operation?" asked the coroner. "Did Mr. Cabral have to switch it off?"

"Yes, of course."

"You know about the alarm systems, presumably?"

"Not the systems in operation now, as the police inspector described them. When Miles and I were married there was a different burglar alarm at the house. It was not connected to the police, but set off a bell on the front wall and a siren in the house. Miles must have changed the installation after I left him."

"So you had keys to the old system, but not to the existing one?"

"I had when I lived there. I sent them back to Miles after we parted."

"Was the discussion between Mr. Cabral, Mr. Roseveare and yourself amicable?"

"I wouldn't say amicable. We were not friends. But it was quite calm and unemotional, if that's what you mean. We didn't have a thundering row."

"Not likely to have contributed to any mental turmoil from which Mr. Cabral might have been suffering?"

"I shouldn't think so," she said. "He treated it as very unimportant—as he always treated anything to do with me."

"You and Mr. Roseveare left the house together, I take it? At what time?"

"About half past four, perhaps a few minutes later."

"Did Mr. Cabral reset the burglar alarm after he had let you out?"

"How would I know?"

"Did you hear a key being turned in the lock in the front door?"

She paused. "Come to think of it, I think I did. Now that you mention it, yes, I did."

The last witness was George Roseveare. He was a heavily-built man, probably in his late thirties; not particularly handsome, his face round and plain; dark hair beginning to recede; thick-rimmed glasses; square, powerful hands that he laid on the edge of the witness stand. He was wearing a formal dark suit, a club tie. The most attractive thing about him was his voice—educated but unaffected, deep in pitch, clear in tone.

He confirmed Miss Hughes's account of what had happened that afternoon. What the coroner wanted, however, was more detail of the business transaction that had taken them there. When the company was formed, Roseveare explained, the directors had given personal guarantees against debt. The debt in question was owed to a finance house in London which, it seemed, had failed to collect it from the company because of some quirk of Guernsey law, and so had turned to the individual directors.

"Was it a substantial debt, Mr. Roseveare?"

"Not for Cabral, I should imagine. But for Miss Hughes, very substantial indeed. It was for rather more than two thousand pounds."

"Did you get the impression that Mr. Cabral was, generally, in financial straits?"

"No. And I'm sure he wasn't."

"Why are you sure?"

"I am in the City myself, sir. If Miles Cabral had been in trouble, it would have been known. But even his suicide set off only a temporary, slight fall in the share values of the companies in which he was involved."

At the end of the hearing the coroner spoke briefly before giving his findings. He was sitting without a jury. He referred to that last remark by Mr. Roseveare as a slip of the tongue. Suicide. The cause of death had not by then been determined. But the coroner could not dispute the term. He had no hesitation, in the light of the evidence, and particularly that of the alarm systems installed in the house, of bringing in a verdict that Miles Cabral killed himself. There was insufficient evidence to add that he did so while the balance of his mind was disturbed. The reason for his death had not been explained, and might never be.

Not so sure of that, Kate murmured to herself.

Henry was at home by the time Kate got back to the flat that evening. He was sprawled in his armchair, surrounded with open books, reading for his latest brief.

"Sorry," she said. "Want me to disappear for a while?"

"No, no. I've had enough of this for today." He started to stack the law books away on their shelf, marking places with slips of paper. "Let's have a drink. Gin?"

While he was fussing with the bottles, the lemon, the ice cubes, she went to the bathroom to clean up and remake her face.

"Ah, lovely," she murmured, taking her drink and easing back into her chair, kicking off her shoes. He had flicked on another bar of the electric heater. Warm. A small flat, up a lot of stairs from the street, but always cosy. In winter she loved it.

"That woman at the inquest, Henry. Angela Hughes. What did you make of her? I thought she was lying."

"I almost agree. Certainly unconvincing. I had the feeling that I could shake her pretty badly if I could cross-examine."

"About that company in Guernsey?"

"Yes. I know their law differs from ours, but we've a Channel Islands précis at the chambers, and I had a look into it this afternoon. There doesn't seem to be any reason why a London finance company cannot collect a genuine debt from an off-shore company registered in Guernsey."

Kate agreed. "I did a little research on that too this afternoon. We've a stringer in St. Peter Port. Nice chap named Jacques. So I phoned him. He knew quite a lot about Cabral's company registered there, because of Cabral's death being in the news. Seems he was well known in the Channel Islands, and Jacques and the other local lads had been doing pieces for their papers and for the news agencies. Though not much was put out on the tapes this afternoon.

"Anyhow, this company. It's a finance and trading outfit —you know, the kind of off-shore company you can register in the Channel Islands. Seems it dealt chiefly in the Middle East. Arab countries, but not Israel. It was linked with a bank of some sort which used to be in Beirut, but since the Lebanese fighting has transferred to Damascus. We've had a reporter in Lebanon for a couple of months, young Geoff Wilton. Don't think you've met him. Anyway, I got him on the line, after a bit of a struggle, and he's going to have a nose around at that end."

Henry demurred, "Isn't that taking rather a lot of trouble over an academic point? Suppose Angela Hughes was lying at the inquest. All that could mean is that she was having a row with Cabral that she didn't want to make public. So she put in this story of the Guernsey company. Did Jacques know, by the way, if she is a director?"

"Yes. From the start. He had been looking it up in their company registry. There were four directors in all, of whom Angela was one. But Jacques said none of them had ever been known over there, except Cabral himself. Obviously he ran the operation and the others were just names, to comply with something or other."

"And you think the operation was crook?" mused Henry. "Could well be. Cabral handled a lot of international business. He could certainly have used an offshore outfit for all sorts of reasons, tax among them."

He got up to refill their glasses.

"But what's the point, Kate? You're not suggesting that there was some great financial scandal about to break, so Cabral shot himself?"

"Not at all. The boot was about to be put in, as you might say, by the other foot. Thanks," she said, taking her drink. "I went down to our City office and talked to Frank."

"The business editor, isn't he?"

"Yes. Runs the business pages. He's been in the City from just about Roman times on, and knows everybody. He knew quite a lot about George Roseveare."

"Such as?"

"It's Roseveare who's on the point of going broke. He's one of the young bloods—county family, father a baronet, played golf for Cambridge—who thought they'd easily make a killing in the property market. So, of course, it went wrong. He got his finance from a small fringe bank. To get it, of course, he put up the deeds of his properties as security. The rumour is, Frank told me, that for a couple of years somebody has been buying up those mortgages from the bank, which was only too pleased to get rid of them, even at a loss. For George Roseveare has become a very bad risk indeed. They think in the City that the man buying those mortgages must have been Cabral."

"Because of Angela Hughes? Rich man's spite?"

Kate nodded. "Frank thinks that Cabral had just about got the lot, and was ready to foreclose and put George and Angela up the creek. I reckon that's what they went to talk to Cabral about that afternoon, not about an offshore company in the Channel Islands. I told you I had the feeling that the woman was lying. She wasn't doing it very well. Awkward at it."

"Normally honest people usually are," Henry conceded. "But why should Cabral have agreed to talk to them about it? If he'd got Roseveare on the scaffold, why talk? All he had to do was pull the lever."

Kate agreed. She had had the same doubt. But Frank had an answer to that too.

"Frank has a pal, a business columnist on one of the Sunday papers. He wouldn't tell me which. He and this chap were having a drink together, and the talk got around to the Roseveare situation. It was something that the City boys were all rather amused about, a bit spicy, dramatic. Divorced husband kicks ex-wife's lover in the groin, to paraphrase the way they would put it. Not just the normal business story, but a bit of human interest."

"So?"

"So the Sunday man told Frank it might not be as simple as they thought. It seems he was also a pal of George Roseveare. And George had been dropping hints that he might come up with a really juicy piece of information about Miles Cabral. Of course, it could have been a frightened man cooking up a few illusions to comfort himself. But . . ."

Henry motioned to her to stop.

"I'd like to get clear what you are suggesting. You think, don't you, that Roseveare had some information which gave him a hold over Cabral? So Angela phoned her ex-husband that lunch-time and gave him an idea of what could be in store. That would certainly be a reason for Cabral to agree to see them."

"And for something more?"

"No. That won't do, darling. Cabral didn't have to shoot himself in despair. All he had to do was to give Roseveare his mortgages back—buy his way out. Assuming that there was anything worth paying to get out from."

"I wasn't thinking of suicide," she said.

"Oh, come on Kate, let's go out and eat," said Henry, getting up to pour one more drink. "Otherwise you'll go on theorizing wildly all the evening. And it simply isn't on. Angela and her boy-friend might have gone to Cabral's house to threaten him with something, to stop him ruining them both. I grant you that possibility—probability if you like. But they did not shoot him. They could not have got out of the house afterwards. The only alarm keys—the only available alarm keys, old Comfort is satisfied about that—were still in Cabral's trousers pocket."

"She knew the house," objected Kate. "She had lived there. Suppose she was lying when she said there had been a different alarm in her time, and in fact she still had keys."

"I'll get your coat, Kate. Do you think for a moment that Chief Inspector Comfort hasn't checked on the date the present system was installed? It's on record in Scotland Yard itself. Give up, duckie. It's simply not possible."

CHAPTER 7

Since Henry was dining in hall at his Inn a couple of evenings later, Kate stayed on at the office. When the night news desk arrived, she went across to the Scriveners, the pub down the alley on the other side of the street, for a couple of gins with Butch and a few of the subs. They drifted away one by one, Butch leaving last. Was she meeting Henry, he asked? No. Henry was eating with his legal chums, and heaven knew how long that would go on into the night. She would have a bite here, to save the bother of cooking herself something at home.

"Good night, then," said Butch.

Kate asked Mrs. Jeffs, behind the bar, for a bowl of hot soup followed by a plate of cold ham and beef and a jacket-baked potato split for a pat of melting butter. She took half a pint of bitter to drink with it. By the time she had finished it was nearly nine o'clock.

As she stepped out into the alley she was glad of that hot soup and the potato. The night was raw. In the street lights at the end of the alley she could see thin rain slanting down. She shivered and pulled up the collar of her coat.

She did not notice the man in the dark doorway until he jumped out as she passed and hit her.

The first blow caught her on the back of the neck. The second, across her face, sent her flat into the wet, muddy gutter. She was almost too surprised to scream. As she lay there she had a sharp glimpse of the man—young, dark-skinned, dressed in sweater and jeans. He was running off towards the street. Then she screamed for help. He turned momentarily to glance back at her, then ran on.

Her cries brought a couple of men from the public bar of the Scriveners. They helped her up. By now she was sobbing with pain, and conscious of the blood running down her face. Through the mist of it all she recognized her helpers, men from the machine room at the *Post*.

They recognized her too. What had happened?

"I got mugged."

One of the men picked up her handbag from the gutter. "Good job we came out sharp, Kate. Disturbed him before he could grab your bag."

"Look after her, Jack," said the other, "while I get a taxi."

Jack supported her as the other hastened towards the lights of the street.

"Don't worry," he told her. "We'll get you to Bart's, so they can have a look at you."

"I'm not badly hurt," she protested.

But when the other man called from the end of the alley, and Jack helped her out to the taxi, she was not sorry to be taken to Casualty at the hospital. The machine-room men had to get back to the presses. She'd be looked after all right now. She nodded, thanking them.

They soon fixed her up in Casualty. There was a nasty cut on her lip, but most of the blood came from the blow on her nose and had now dried up.

"Nothing serious," the young doctor assured her. "Who mugged you? One of our coloured citizens?"

"I'm not sure. I caught only a glimpse of him, and it was dark in the alley. He was foreign-looking but I don't think he was black."

"Just lie there and rest for half an hour," said the doctor. "Have you far to go?"

"Only to Chelsea."

"I'll tell one of the porters to get you a taxi in half an hour's time."

She murmured her thanks and lay back on the bed, grateful for the tranquilliser he had given her.

The hospital porter had to wake her to tell her a taxi was waiting.

"I tried to clean your coat up," he said as he helped her into it. "But it's still muddy."

"I'll send it to the cleaner's." Looking round, she saw that the nurse was busy and the doctor had gone. "Thank them for me," she asked the porter.

Outside the streets were now streaming with rain. She got stiffly into the taxi, conscious of the ache in her shoulders. The driver looked a sympathetic query.

"Got mugged," she told him.

"Bastards."

To her relief, Henry was home. As she came in, he jumped from his chair in dismay. "What on earth . . . ?"

"Got mugged."

"Oh, darling . . ." He took hold of her consolingly. "Tell me."

She told him of the attack, the hospital.

"It was so pointless. He didn't even get my handbag. It fell in the gutter, and the men from the machine room came running out before he could pick it up."

He helped her get to bed. "Want anything? Aspirin? Whisky?"

"No. The hospital gave me a tranquillizer. I'm still sleepy."

Next morning she felt all right. After a long soak in the bath her shoulders were easier, and when she took the plaster from her lip the cut was nothing much, not so bad as she had feared. But Henry insisted she stay home all day. He brought a breakfast tray to her in bed.

"Will you be all right alone? I have to be in court this morning."

"Of course. I only got mugged. It happens all over London, all the time."

When he had gone she rang the office and got through to Butch. He was all commiseration. "Take a few days off, Kate."

"I'll be in tomorrow. I'm all right. Any messages?"

"Only some woman telephoning for you. She wouldn't give a name. She rang three times this morning. The third time, she said to tell you she had warned you. Mean anything to you?"

"Woman with a foreign accent?"

"Yes."

"She's just a nut. She rang me before. Doesn't mean a thing."

But when she had hung up, she shivered a little. The woman must have known she had been attacked in that alley. So it wasn't an ordinary mugging. That was why she still had her handbag. The youth had had plenty of time, she thought, to grab it from the gutter.

But why? The only piece she'd had in the paper was her report of the Cabral inquest. All the papers carried that, so what was so special about her piece? But there was something. She had added a few details about that company registered in Guernsey, the information she had got from Jacques in St. Peter Port.

She found the clipping, to check her memory of what exactly she had added. Chiefly it was about the activities of the Guernsey company—that it dealt mostly wtih the Middle East and that it had been linked with a bank in Beirut which had been transferred to Damascus because of the conflict in Lebanon.

Kate recalled her impression of the woman's accent over the phone; possibly from somewhere in the Middle East.

When she returned to the office tomorrow she would phone Geoff Wilton again in Beirut, to learn if he had uncovered anything.

But one thing was certain. She would say nothing of this to Henry. He panicked about her so easily.

There was no need to phone Wilton in Beirut. He had filed a service message to her relating all he had been able to discover.

Butch, of course, was curious. What was it all about? Kate put him off with a reference to the off-shore company in Guernsey and its link with a bank in Damascus. Butch was unsatisfied, but she insisted there was nothing more as yet to tell.

Kate took the message to her desk and worked through the telegraphese. There were no records in Beirut of the bank in which she was interested. But the town had been so heavily shelled and shattered that most records had been destroyed; and Beirut was not noted anyway for keeping records of financial transactions.

Geoff had not been to Damascus. He would go if she wanted, but he had found a former cashier of the bank who, for a consideration, had spilled quite a lot about it.

Cabral had gone there three or four times a year and, when there, seemed in control. The cashier was not certain, but thought Cabral owned the bank. By far the bulk of the business it transacted was his. Large sums were frequently paid into his account, usually in sterling, U.S. dollars, Deutschmarks or Swiss francs. The sterling always came through Cabral's company in the Channel Islands. So did quite a lot of the other currency inputs, though some were paid direct into the Beirut bank.

The money was never kept long in Lebanon, but was transferred either to a Swiss bank or, more often, to a bank in the United States.

The only other major account handled by the little bank was that of a Beiruti named Fouad Hakim, a silversmith who had a small workshop in a poor quarter of the city; he also used to buy his precious metals through the bank while it was still in Beirut.

Hakim and Cabral were business associates—the ex-cashier did not know the nature of the business—and always met on Cabral's visits. When Cabral was in London, he sometimes sent a courier to Hakim, presumably carrying business documents. The courier's name was Sharp.

Wilton had been to the silversmith's workshop—remarkably still standing in that shell-battered district of the town —and had seen the man. But he had shut the door in his face, refusing to say anything.

With a little mental whistle of astonishment, Kate locked the message in her desk and went out to take a taxi to the Cabral house off Eaton Square.

*

First she tried the door to the basement flat, but nobody answered. Nor was there any response to the bell of the front door of the house. Kate was just deciding that Fred Sharp must be at Cabral's Sussex place, when she saw him coming along the street.

"Can't get in there, missus," he said. "Mr. Comfort got me to show him how to work the perimeter alarm, then he locked the house up and took the guv'nor's keys, as well as mine to the front door."

"I don't want to get in. It was you I came to see."

"About something, then?" he asked cautiously.

"I went to see Mr. Grogan, as you asked me to."

"Ah," he said, leading the way down the steps into the area. "Come on in, then."

It was so dark in the little front room of the basement flat that he switched on the light. The room was sparsely furnished, but clean. Fred Sharp offered Kate the arm-chair and, after removing his long black overcoat, sat on the sofa.

"It was worth while going to see Mr. Grogan," Kate began. "He told me how his enquiries led to a young girl named Rosemary Ward. Did you know about her, Mr. Sharp?"

"Saw her once or twice," he admitted uneasily. "Lovely girl."

"Very attractive."

"You found her then, missus?"

"She's living with a young actor, Jonathan Parr, at Clapham. Did you know that he and Mr. Cabral had one hell of a row one night, at a party in the Kensington flat where he was keeping Rosemary?"

"Heard something about it."

Kate wondered why he seemed so wary.

"And next day Mr. Cabral threw Rosemary out?"

"The guv'nor didn't keep girls for long. Didn't hold with it."

"Mr. Sharp, why did you ask me to go to see Mr. Grogan?"

When he said nothing, she went on, "I'll tell you what I think. You said there were things going on that you couldn't tell me about. They were Mr. Cabral's business. But the things going on could be a reason for somebody wanting to kill Mr. Cabral. Did you mean Jonathan Parr—because of Rosemary, and because of the coins Cabral had tricked her into letting him have, she not knowing how valuable they were?

"Is that what you meant, Mr. Sharp? Did you hope I would keep on asking questions, until I would find out that Jonathan somehow got into and out of this house that afternoon, shot Mr. Cabral and took back the coins? If he did, he certainly hasn't returned them to Rosemary, or even told her anything about them.

"Well, was that why you wanted me to go to see the private detective Mr. Cabral had hired?"

The man said nothing.

"You knew, didn't you, that even if Jonathan shot your boss, he didn't get those coins back? They weren't there, were they?"

"What coins, missus? I don't know what you're talking about."

"Pennies dated 1933 and 1954, and an Edward VIII threepenny piece."

The wary look was back in his eyes now. He muttered, "So you know. You must've got it from that actor chap. So he must've known too."

"Yes, he knew. What he didn't know was that you had carried them to Lebanon for Mr. Cabral, to deliver them to a silversmith named Fouad Hakim, to sell them discreetly on a world market without ever involving Mr. Cabral at all."

Sharp shook his head. "You got it wrong. I didn't take them coins anywhere. And I don't know nothing about anyone called Hakim. Okay, so Mr. Cabral had them coins. But they wasn't taken when he was shot. Somebody'd stolen them earlier that day."

Kate, startled, asked, "How do you know?"

"Not for sure. But I put two and two together, missus." He hesitated. "If I tell you something, it's not for printing in your paper."

"No, Mr. Sharp. That's an old trick, and I don't fall for it. I never accept any information in confidence. If you want to tell me, you have to leave it to me to decide whether or not I print it."

His face was pale. He sat in silence for a few moments. His tongue nervously licked his dry lips.

"Okay," he said at last. "It's what the guv'nor phoned me to bring to London that day. Tools."

"Tools?" she asked, puzzled.

"Breaking and entering, missus. Okay, I got a record. But that was before I worked for Mr. Cabral. Okay, I done a few jobs for him, on the quiet. Not stealing, missus. Only getting back papers or documents or something he wanted from other people. So when he phoned that day, I knew he'd want me to get something out of somebody else's place for him. Must've been them coins."

Kate was trying to work it out. "You mean, somebody had stolen the coins some time before, and Mr. Cabral knew where they were, and wanted you to break in and recover them for him? How could they have been stolen from this house at any time?"

"Might not've been from this house, missus. Maybe the guv'nor had the coins with him. And it must've been they were nicked the same day."

"Why?"

"Because he drives up from Sussex in the morning, and never says nothing about it. If the coins'd been done by then, he'd have brought me with him. But he phones me in the afternoon, and says come up and bring your things. So the coins must've been done that day earlier."

"You're just guessing, aren't you?"

"Sure. But what else? The guv'nor phones me to come up and get something for him. What's missing is them coins. So what else?"

"You think it was Jonathan Parr who took them for Rosemary," she asked, "and Mr. Cabral knew, and you were to break into that bed-sitter while they were both at the theatre, and get them back?"

"Could've been him. Could've been anyone what was around that day. But he seems likely, don't he?"

"Not to me," Kate answered. "For one thing, we don't know that the coins were stolen at all. For another, it seems unlikely that Jonathan Parr was there that day. What time in the day? Mr. Cabral drove up from Sussex and spent all morning at the auction. He lunched at his club. Angela Hughes said at the inquest that she telephoned him there. He didn't get back to this securely locked house until ten past four, because Angela Hughes and George Roseveare were waiting outside and saw him arrive in his car. What time did Mr. Cabral phone you in Sussex?"

"About half after two. He said to get up here that evening. He'd not want me till evening. Not till it were dark," he added with a grim sort of smile.

Kate gazed at him for a moment, then decided to try the classic interview tactic—snap out the vital question suddenly, unexpectedly.

"All those times you went to Lebanon as Mr. Cabral's courier, what did you carry?"

He stiffened. "You're talking daft, missus. I was the guv'nor's manservant, not his—what did you call it?— carrier. I didn't carry nothing for him, no place."

"I work for a newspaper, Mr. Sharp. We have stringers —local journalists who work for us when asked—all over the world. I asked our stringer in the Channel Islands to ferret around Mr. Cabral's finance company in Guernsey, and he came across its link with a small bank in Beirut, which has now moved to Damascus. It happens that, because of the civil war, we sent a staff reporter to Lebanon."

"What's that, then? This Lebanon place?"

"I asked him to see what he could discover about the Cabral bank. This morning I had a long report from him. Mr. Cabral went there now and then. You made quite a lot of trips, over the years, sometimes to the bank, sometimes to a silversmith named Fouad Hakim, who has a workshop in Beirut. So what were you carrying for Mr. Cabral?"

"I ain't saying nothing."

"Why not? There's nothing to hide, is there? You weren't carrying currency for him. He did all his illegal sterling exporting through Guernsey. My guess is that Mr. Cabral was not only a coin collector, but a coin dealer. He didn't want that to get out publicly, because of his business reputation, so he used this silversmith as his agent to sell rare coins on the world collectors' market, mostly in Switzerland, West Germany and the United States. You carried the coins out to Hakim and saw that he put the proceeds into the little bank in Beirut. Good guess?"

"Guess what you wants to, missus," said Fred Sharp sullenly. "I got things to do. You got to go now."

In her taxi on the way back to the office, Kate pondered about timing. Why had Cabral phoned Fred in Sussex at half past two in the afternoon, telling him to come to London that evening prepared for a little burglary?

It could have had nothing to do with the coins. At that time, Cabral had not been to his London house that day at all. What it followed was his ex-wife's telephone call to him at his club at lunch-time, when he agreed, surprisingly, to see her and George Roseveare at his house at four o'clock that afternoon. The likelihood was that the house that Fred Sharp was to burgle was George and Angela's pad, wherever that was.

But what was Fred to recover? It had to be something that Cabral wanted pretty badly. Kate's thoughts went back to the City rumours which Frank had passed on to her—that George Roseveare had been hinting to a Sunday-newspaper financial columnist that there would soon be a juicy scandal that could ruin Cabral.

So George had proof of some sort of activity by Cabral that, if known, would put him in trouble—probably in gaol. Perhaps it was proof that he had been illegally exporting large sums in sterling. There would have to be papers—documents, sworn statements, and so on. Those were what Fred Sharp was to break in for.

So what happened at that afternoon meeting in Cabral's house? George and Angela produced their proof; photocopies, no doubt. The originals would be handed over to Cabral if he cancelled George's debts; property finance

could run into a huge sum. Cabral must have demanded
how he could be sure that, if he complied, George had not
kept other photocopies. Angela had answered that if
George then produced other copies he would be exposing
himself to a criminal charge of blackmail.

Kate reckoned that Cabral probably pretended to comply, to string them along. That night, Fred Sharp would get
the documents anyway, and all the copies, and George
Roseveare could be bankrupted. If Fred failed, Cabral's
position would not have worsened. He would have to think
of some other way.

Kate would pay another call on Frank in the City office,
she decided. If Frank asked around quietly, he could come
up with most of the information she wanted.

Back in the office she carefully re-read Geoff Wilton's
message from Beirut. In the light of it, and now that she
had seen Fred Sharp, she was farly sure that those three
coins had not been stolen at all. Either Fred was lying,
and he had taken them out to Fouad Hakim, or perhaps
Cabral had made the journey himself.

So, with the utmost discretion, and probably at intervals
over a long period, the coins would be sold to three very
wealthy numismatists, none knowing of the existence of the
two other coins. Probably Hakim would pick customers
with whom he had made shady deals previously, in different countries; one in America perhaps, one in Switzerland
and one in Germany.

Cornelius Ball, it suddenly struck her, might well have
been a Hakim customer in the past, and perhaps knew he
was Cabral's under-cover agent. That could have been why
Ball was so anxious to know whether the 1954 penny was
still in Cabral's London collection. She smiled at the recol-
lection of the ease with which that suave ex-ambassador
had gently extracted from her the one piece of information he wanted; all those enquiries about Cabral's
women had been simply camouflage. Ball was by now
probably in touch with the silversmith in Beirut. He could
even already have bought the penny.

Butch called to her from the news desk. "Here's something to interest you, Kate."

He handed her a Reuters message that had just come in.
A claim to Miles Cabral's estate, expected to run into several
million pounds, had been filed in the New York courts by
Mr. Cornelius Ball, the millionaire ex-ambassador.

He was claiming the estate, not for himself but for his infant nephew, the son of his late sister, Miss Ursula Ball. The claim was that she had been Miles Cabral's common-law wife, and the baby, named Cedric, was his son.

CHAPTER 8

Kate turned to the news-desk secretary. "Bertha, who's doing the publicity for the play Angela Hughes is in?"

Bertha turned up the list. "Larry Corcoran."

"Can you get him on the line and put him through to my desk? Make me sound a bit unimportant?"

"Sure."

"Hallo Larry," said Kate when the call came through. "I've got a break for you. I'll interview Angela Hughes."

"Because of her ex-husband?"

"Naturally. She's in the news. What I have in mind is a profile."

"The play gets named?"

"Of course."

"Super. I'll fix it. When do you want to see her?"

"Larry, the *Post* is a daily newspaper. Whatever we want, we want it today."

"There's a matinée today. I can probably arrange it between that and the evening performance. I'll call you back."

Ten minutes later he was on the phone again. "In her dressing-room after the matinée. She needs a little time to get her paint off. Can you be there at half past five? Super. Stage door, of course. I'll tell Billy."

At the appointed time Kate took a bus to Piccadilly and walked up Shaftesbury Avenue. Billy was almost a caricature of a stage-doorkeeper—in his shirtsleeves, wearing a bowler hat, with the stub of a hand-rolled cigarette stuck to his lower lip. He gestured her through to Miss Hughes's dressing-room.

She was seated at the usual dressing-table before a large triple mirror stuck around with electric lamps. Her dresser, the usual elderly body in black, was hanging her stage clothes behind a curtain. A gilt armchair had been set for Kate alongside the table, on which stood a tea tray. "Unless you'd prefer a drink," said Angela.

"No. I'd love a cup of tea."

"Usual time this evening then, Mrs. Jenkins," said Angela to the dresser, who put on her hat and coat and left.

"You haven't come about the play, of course," said Angela, pouring the tea and passing over a plate of sugared biscuits.

"I made that clear to Larry Corcoran. I hope he told you."

"Not he. But of course I didn't have to be told. You've come about Miles."

"Thanks," said Kate, taking her teacup. Excellent tea; Earl Grey, she thought. "Not about Miles. About you. You're in the news, and my job includes interviewing people in the news. I promised Larry I'd name the play, and I'll put in anything else you want about your stage career."

Angela smiled sadly. "A row of middling performances in second-rate comedies. Nothing I want about that. Once George and I are married, I'm going to chuck the theatre. So what do you want?"

Kate instinctively liked this woman. Close to, her age showed more clearly; probably nearer forty than thirty-five. And she looked tired. But it was an intelligent face, her eyes were calm, she gave the impression of quality.

"I'll be absolutely frank," Kate told her, suddenly deciding her tactic. "Why did you cook up that story at the inquest of the debt and the finance company in Guernsey?"

"I suppose I ought to resent that remark. Miles has— or I should say had—a finance company in Guernsey, and he did make me a director of it when we were still married. I simply don't know if I'm still on the board. The debt, as you correctly surmise, was a fabrication."

"So why?"

"Do you know, I don't think I'm going to tell you, Mrs. Theobald."

"Kate is simpler. Do you mind if I try to tell you?"

Angela smiled but said nothing.

"George Roseveare's situation is pretty well known in the City, at any rate to City journalists. The *Post* man is probably the most knowledgeable of all. So what I hear is that Mr. Roseveare's bid for a property empire having foundered, as did so many others, he was more than a little vulnerable to anybody who chose to take over his bank debts. Which is what Miles Cabral did. They think in the

City that out of pure spite, because of you—injured pride, if you like, of an egomaniac—Miles Cabral was on the point of foreclosing and finishing Roseveare off. Some were even wondering in the City whether a bankruptcy might disclose a few irregularities that could put Roseveare in the dock at the Old Bailey."

"That bit's not true," said Angela in a quiet voice. "I would not contradict the rest."

"Some more City gossip has it that George Roseveare has been hinting to a journalist whom he knew well that there might be a juicy scandal involving Cabral. Could even put *him* in the dock."

"Gossip in the City must be worse than in the theatre."

"So George had discovered something really damaging to Miles. When you phoned him at his club at lunchtime, you gave him an idea of what it was, and offered a deal—cancellation of George's debts against surrender of whatever it was that could incriminate Miles. Correct?"

Angela smiled sweetly. "Sounds more convincing, I must admit, than the Guernsey business."

"Did you do a deal, Angela?"

"The idea that we proposed one is yours, not mine."

"You would have to have had written proof. And I guess you were careless enough to keep it in your flat, or house, or wherever you and George are living."

"Flat in Knightsbridge. So that's what you think."

"It's what your ex-husband thought. He had made arrangements to have your flat burgled while you were at the theatre that evening."

For the first time the woman was startled. "You can't really mean that."

"Immediately after you phoned him at his club, and must have threatened him with something serious, or he wouldn't have let you come to his house, he phoned a man he has who's a skilled burglar. Miles told him to bring his tools along to his house—jemmy, or whatever he needed—after it got dark. There was a job for him that evening."

"I was never particularly sorry that Miles shot himself," said Angela softly. "Now I'm glad."

"If he did," remarked Kate off hand.

"But he did. Oh, I see. You mean perhaps somebody shot him. Surely not a possibility inside that burglar alarm." She made a little grimace. "There were certainly plenty of aspirants to that part in the play. Me for one, you could say. George certainly. George would cheerfully have despatched him by slow strangulation."

"And Cornelius Ball?" asked Kate.

Angela stared at her. After a pause, she said, "You seem very well informed."

"No secret about the source of that information. I had it from Mr. Ball himself."

"From Cornelius? How?"

"When he was in London, just after it had all happened, he asked me to lunch at the Connaught. Delicious, it was. I think what he really wanted to find out was whether Miles had a 1954 penny. I'd mentioned it in my piece in the *Post* that morning. But he covered that up by pretending he was really interested in what lay behind something I had written about the women who might contest his will. He spoke of you, and said that you and his sister Ursula were great friends, had been together at Oxford, and he first met Miles through you." A sudden idea came to her. "Was it Mr. Ball who gave you the information with which to offer Miles a deal?"

Angela nodded. "When he learned what Miles was going to do to George—you were right about that—Cornelius came to see me. He told me things about Miles that I'd never dreamed of, and backed it all up with certain papers, letters and so on. If that didn't do the trick, Cornelius said, he would let me have more. He hated Miles so much that he had spent months trying to get something on him. And he had got plenty. He had even been out to the Middle East, where he had once been an ambassador, and so still had contacts. He knew that Miles had some business concerns out there."

"He hated him so much because of his sister Ursula?" asked Kate.

Angela gazed at her. "Did Cornelius tell you of that?"

"A little. Not much."

"It's an old story," said Angela evasively, "and a sad one, and there's no point in recalling it now that Miles is dead."

"Cornelius Ball seems to be reviving it himself," Kate told her. She handed her a copy of the Reuters message from New York. "That came into the office today."

As she read the copy, Angela bit on the forefinger of her

left hand, as though to stifle emotion. When she looked up again at Kate there were tears in her eyes.

"If I'd known," she murmured. "If only I'd known, I would have tried to stop him. How awful—to bring it all out into the open."

"It could be a vast fortune for the child."

"What would Cedric want with more money than Cornelius will leave him? Why, oh why did he do it? Miles is dead. To blacken him after his death . . . Can hate make you do that?"

"If it's fierce enough, maybe."

"He and Ursula were so close, until Miles got her. She was much younger than he. Their parents were killed in an air crash when she was a child. So Cornelius brought her up. He was a sort of father to her as well as brother. Then, when it started with Miles, Ursula cut loose from him, because he wouldn't accept. In a way, I was responsible. It was through me . . ."

She tailed off. So the idea came to Kate. "Was it because of Ursula that you divorced Miles?"

"That was somebody else, just sordid. Ursula went to him after we were apart. But it was through me that she and Cornelius first came to know him. And then she was infatuated. I tried to warn her, but she wouldn't listen. I told her that when he got tired of her he would throw her out. She didn't believe it."

"Did he ditch her because there was a child coming?"

"Maybe. I don't know. By then she was not telling me anything. We never quarrelled. I was still her friend—her only friend, I think." She stopped suddenly. "Why should I tell you all this?"

"It's bound to come out in the court hearing in New York."

"I suppose so. How I wish he hadn't done it."

"So Ursula didn't come to you when Miles threw her out?" asked Kate gently.

"No. She just went away, and nobody seemed to know where. In fact she had gone to France and hidden herself in a small village in Brittany. She'd been there once before, on a painting trip. She was a Sunday painter. She knew a farmer, and lodged with his family. She had her child there. It was only after that I had a sudden phone call, to come to her, please to come to her. I went that hour.

As it happened, I wasn't working then. If I had been, I'd have thrown up the play.

"She was ill, desperately ill. The birth had been bungled —some filthy old village midwife. I phoned Cornelius. I made her give me his number in New York, and mercifully he was there. He caught the next plane to Paris, hired a car and drove like a demon. He was too late. She died an hour before he got there."

"Did Miles know?"

"Yes. When everything had been settled in France, Cornelius went to London and faced him with it. Miles simply laughed. His child? Could have been his, perhaps, but maybe not—not with a promiscuous slut for a mother. That was a lie, of course, and both of them knew it; said simply to wound. Cornelius nearly hit him. But he controlled himself, he told me, in case, if he started, he might go on until he killed him. He told Miles that he would get him, some way or another, if it took the rest of his life. Cornelius had hated him ever since he seduced Ursula in the first place. That was when the outbidding at auctions started. It became quite notorious. But after Ursula died . . ."

"Cornelius did discover enough to get Miles?"

"Cornelius is very rich, and he spent thousands to get it. I knew nothing of that until, when I discovered what Miles was going to do to George, I wrote to Cornelius in desperation. He came to London straight away, and gave me certain papers which he said would be enough to force Miles to leave George alone."

"Proof of illegal exporting of currency through that company in Guernsey?"

"Vast sums. And if that wasn't enough, Cornelius said, he would give me plenty more ammunition. That was what he must have faced Miles with that day, told him what was coming to him, drove him to shoot himself . . ."

"Faced him that day?" asked Kate, startled. "You mean he was in that house that afternoon? His tale of not getting any response was untrue?"

Angela sat up sharply in her chair, her hands clenching the edge of the dressing-table, the fingers white. Her eyes opened wide, almost as though she were coming out of a trance.

"Of course I don't mean that. I don't know what he did. How would I know? None of this is for your newspaper."

"Don't worry. The editor doesn't fancy going to gaol for criminal libel."

Angela got up, looking down at her uncertainly. "I have your promise?"

"No reporter ever gives that promise. But don't worry."

Pale, almost trembling, Angela declared, "If you write anything I've told you, I shall deny having said it. You couldn't prove any of it, Please go now. Please don't write anything about me, or the play. I agreed to your interview only because Larry said the publicity might help save it. It's on the point of closing, and they'll all be out of work, and unemployment in the theatre . . . Promise me not to write."

Kate stood up. "No promises. Sorry. But as I said, don't worry. I couldn't possibly print anything you've told me about Cornelius and how he hated Miles. So don't worry."

But she was certainly going to worry like hell, Kate told herself on the way out past Billy and through the stage door. There was a bill of the play posted on the back wall of the theatre. Kate idly read it, the names of the wretches who would soon be out of work . . .

She drew in her breath sharply. Near the bottom of the cast list was the name Jonathan Parr.

Back in the office, Kate asked Butch if there were anything more about Cornelius Ball and the suit filed for the baby.

He detached some copy from the spike. "Only a service message from Lewis in New York. Ball has gone to earth somewhere. None of the men out there can find him. Nobody knows where the baby is, or when he was brought to America, if he ever was. No registration of the birth that any of them can find, or of the sister's death."

"Just negative," murmured Kate.

She sat at her desk, pondering. Then suddenly she thought . . . Possible? Worth a try anyway. She called across for Larry Corcoran's number. Luckily he was still at his office.

"Larry, I had a most interesting interview with Angela Hughes. Many thanks."

"Super."

"I'm going to hold up my piece for a little, because she said I should see her country cottage to get a true picture of her—the life she really loves, not the theatre. So I'll go down tomorrow. But I'm not sure I've got the address right."

"Hang on," he said. After a pause he came back. "Blue-bell Cottage, Mill Lane, Catsfield."

"Sussex, isn't it?"

"Near Battle."

"Thanks, Larry."

She would have to remember to tell him tomorrow that Angela had changed her mind and asked her not to print the interview.

She told the news-desk secretary, "Get me an office car, please, right away. The driver may have to stay out most of the night. And in about an hour, would you please ring my home and tell Henry I'm off on an enquiry and may not be back until after midnight?"

The driver—Sam, who had often driven her before, thank goodness—knew his way to Battle all right. By then the night was black and it was raining heavily. They stopped at the George for sandwiches and beer, and Sam enquired the way to the cottage.

"Bit remote," he said, "but we'll find it."

Remote it was. The turning into the lane was narrow and Sam missed it the first time and had to turn back. The cottage lay a few yards off the lane, behind a thicket of shrubs, with a black line of trees beyond. But there was light in the downstairs windows.

"Wait here, Sam. Probably won't be for long. I'll likely get the door slammed on me."

"Take your time," he assured her, lighting a cigarette.

She turned up the collar of her coat and ran through the rain. Luckily the cottage door was sheltered in a porch.

The woman who answered was plain, middle-aged, looked kindly, amiable; but somewhat startled.

"My name's Kate Theobald. I write for the *Post*." Kate showed her Press card. "I've been interviewing Miss Hughes, and she said I should come to see Cedric."

For a moment she thought she had guessed wrong. But then the woman said, though doubtfully, "Then you'd bet-ter come in, miss. Have you got a car?"

She peered into the dark.

"In the lane. The driver's waiting." Kate stepped inside. "I take it you're looking after the baby."

"That's right, miss. He's asleep now, of course, but I suppose you could take a peep at him."

"Tell me about him first," suggested Kate, following the woman into the living-room; charming, very old, dark oak beams, a small ingle, logs smouldering on the glowing ash in the fire basket.

As they entered the room a man rose from a chair by the fireside.

"Come in, Mrs. Theobald. Let me take your coat, and sit here to get warm," said Cornelius Ball. "Did Angela really send you to see the baby?"

"No. I guessed. A long shot, of course, and you weren't part of the guess."

"Well, really . . ." put in the nanny.

"It's all right, Mrs. Horton. Mrs. Theobald and I know each other. Can I get you a drink, or some food?"

"No, thanks. We stopped off in Battle for sandwiches and beer. But I really have been interviewing Angela Hughes, and she did tell me about the baby, and your sister's death. I'm very sorry."

The nanny murmured something about seeing to something or other and tactfully went out of the room.

Cornelius Ball sat on a settle on the other side of the ingle.

"It seems to me," he said, "that you are a most enterprising, very clever, and rather dangerous young woman."

"I'm a newspaper reporter."

"That," Ball assented, "is precisely what I mean. Of all this, what are you going to report? About Cedric?"

"Since you filed that suit in New York, he is news."

"If you disclose where he is, this cottage will be besieged. I shall have to move him somewhere else. And I don't want to, Mrs. Theobald. If you link him with Angela, she will be harassed. I'd like to avoid that for her."

Kate reassured him. "I won't mention Angela, or give any clue to this location. Enlightened self-interest, Mr. Ball. I don't want anyone else getting in on my exclusive. I propose to say that the baby was born in France and is now in England. I must give some account of your sister's death. I'm sorry. I don't want to hurt you. But it is bound to come out anyway when your suit is heard in New York. Angela is very distressed, by the way, that you have brought it out into the open by taking that step."

Ball looked troubled. "I feared she would be. I thought very hard and long about it. But the boy has a right to his inheritance. And there seems to be nobody else—no relatives, no other child. I've had enquiries made. Of course, there is Angela. But I will make sure she does not suffer. I am arranging for her claim to be made in your courts. And before there is any hearing of either suit, there will be out-of-court settlements."

"How can you be sure of that?"

"Cabral had very substantial assets in the States, handled by a firm of New York lawyers—real shysters. But my lawyers, when they filed the suit, got an order freezing all Cabral's assets." He smiled. "In the American legal system we can keep them locked in for years. They'll settle out of court for Cedric over there, and I'll wager I get a similar settlement for Angela in London."

"But Miles Cabral has probably willed his money elsewhere," objected Kate.

"Then Angela's and Cedric's lawyers will jointly challenge the will," he replied grimly. "And whoever the other beneficiaries may be, I'm reasonably sure they also will agree to a settlement. Especially when their lawyers get a hint of what could, if necessary, be revealed. Probably Cabral's estate will have to be shared. A compromise, no doubt. I should not object to that. It is not primarily the money we are after—not all of it, anyhow—but acknowledgement."

"Those revelations," asked Kate softly. "They would reveal something damning about Miles Cabral?"

The man's face darkened. Kate suddenly remembered that flash of hatred in his eyes when she had spoken of Cabral's death when she lunched with him.

"He was not only a rogue, Mrs. Theobald. He was a crook, an actual criminal, on a scale that would astonish you."

"What sort of criminal?"

"Evil," was all he would answer. "Evil."

Kate said, "I shall also want to report that you are in England."

Ball resumed his courteous manner. "If you wish. It will not disturb me, Mrs. Theobald. I am simply passing through. I arrived in London two days ago, and came down here to see Cedric. Mrs. Horton has been looking after me. I leave tomorrow, for—for somewhere further on."

"For the Middle East?"

"You must not expect an old and experienced fish like myself to rise to that sort of baited question."

"To Damascus," she asked, "to enquire further about Cabral's bank that has moved there? Or to Beirut to question the agent who sold his rare coins, the silversmith Fouad Hakim?"

At that he looked grave. "Please be guided by me. I am astonished that you know about that, but I beg you not to enquire any further into it. That could be immensely dangerous—dangerous for you. There are things at stake of proportions that I am sure you do not realize. There are people involved who would do anything to protect themselves. People who, shall I say, do not put much value on human life. I am not being dramatic, I assure you."

He stood up.

"Now, Mrs. Theobald, you have that drive back to London. And you came to see Cedric."

He opened the door to the next room and called, "Mrs. Horton, please show Mrs. Theobald the child."

The nanny came back and led Kate up narrow, twisting stairs to a little room lit only by a nightlight, a thickness of candle floating in a saucer of water.

The baby was sleeping peacefully in a curtained cot, his arms arched on the pillow over his head. Kate peered, smiling happily at Mrs. Horton, murmuring how lovely the boy looked.

When she re-entered the living-room to leave the cottage, Cornelius Ball was no longer there.

The rain had eased a little as she dashed for the car.

"Back to the George in Battle, Sam. I'll buy you a drink to warm you up. You must be chilled to the bone. I'll phone my story through to the office, then back to London."

CHAPTER 9

Henry had been home for about half an hour when the *Post* news desk rang through with the message that Kate had gone off on an enquiry and might not be back until after midnight. He thought of going to his club for supper. But the weather was filthy, and he could usefully put in a few hours on a new brief, so he fried himself a dish of bacon and eggs and opened a half-bottle of his cheapest claret to drink with it. After he had eaten and stacked the crockery in the dishwasher, he pulled down law books from the shelf, settled in his chair with the last glass of claret on a table by his side, and started on the brief.

He had scarcely begun to concentrate when the flat doorbell rang. Muttering damn, he went to answer it.

The woman on the landing was elderly, short, swarthy and rain-soaked.

"Please," she began nervously, "I have come to speak with Mrs. Theobald."

Her accent was foreign but Henry could not quite place it.

"Sorry. She's not in, and I don't expect her until late. I'm Mr. Theobald. Can I help?"

The woman hesitated. Her fingers were fumbling nervously with the fringe of a heavy shawl draped over her head.

"She is not in?"

She looked so distressed—and so wet—that Henry suggested she should come in and tell him what she wanted, leave a message for his wife. She started back at first, but then seemed to be forcing herself to step into the flat. Henry took her sodden shawl and thin overcoat and showed her into the living-room, settled her in a chair by the electric heater and switched on an extra element.

"I'll hang these wet things in the kitchen," he said.

When he returned, the old woman seemed calmer, though her fingers were still folding and unfolding little pleats in her long black skirt.

"Now then, Mrs. er . . ."

"Hakim," she said.

"Ah, you are from one of the Arab countries that is driving us into bankruptcy," he joked, laughing a little, trying to make her easier.

"From Lebanon. I am here with my grandson, because of the trouble there. We are not Muslim, but Christian."

"And how can my wife help you, Mrs. Hakim?"

"It is my grandson." She was staring down at her knees and mumbling so hesitantly that Henry could only just make out what she was saying. "He is wild boy."

"My wife knows him?"

"No, no. Not knows him." She suddenly raised her head and looked directly at Henry. She was trembling, in distress. "Oh sir, your wife must stop."

"Stop what?"

"This about Mr. Cabral, now he is dead. If she not stop, there are people who will be angry, very angry. Then my grandson . . . He does not know I am come here. He must not know. I am worried to my grave for him, for what he might do. I cannot tell him, he will not talk with me about these things. So I am desperate, sir. So I thought I could explain to Mrs. Theobald, she would understand, and not report any more about it."

"Why not explain to me? Then I can explain to my wife."

"These people, very strong and angry people. Not my grandson. But he will obey, that is my terror. He will do what they tell him. So please, Mrs. Theobald should stop reporting more about Mr. Cabral, now he is dead."

"Why are these people angry?" asked Henry.

"Because . . . because . . . I cannot tell you. But it must not be known, not reported about. Myself, I do not know all these things. But I know these people angry. Not my grandson, but he is wild . . ."

Henry began to wonder if the old woman were a little touched in the head, one of the cranks that newspapers seem to attract. Kate had occasionally been troubled by people of that sort. She always laughed about it; quite harmless, not to worry, only to be sorry for them.

The old woman was easing herself up from the chair, the way an arthritic moves.

"Stay a little longer," he said, "and warm yourself."

"No. I must go now. I think I am wrong to come. But I am in despair."

"Would you like me to talk to your grandson?"

The look in the woman's eyes was of real terror. "No, no. He must not know. If he knows, he is very angry with me. But I am afraid for him. Your wife, you will stop your wife?"

"I will tell her what you have said."

She turned towards the door. Henry went to fetch her coat and shawl from the kitchen. They were still soaking wet, the poor old thing would surely catch cold.

By now she was in the hall, trying to open the front door.

"Let me phone for a taxi for you, Mrs. Hakim."

"No, no. I go by bus. Number thirty-one."

"But you have to go to the other end of King's Road to catch a thirty-one."

"It is no matter. I must go now."

Henry helped her into her coat. She took the shawl and swathed it over her head.

"Do let me get you a taxi. If it's a question of the fare—" he murmured, feeling in his pocket for a couple of pound notes.

She pushed them back at him. "It is only that you stop your wife."

He opened the door for her. She grasped the handrail and started down the stairs, stiffly, one at a time. He felt anxiously sorry for her. But what could he do? He closed the door and returned to his books.

Kate got home earlier than he had expected, not much after eleven. What a lousy night to be out in, she complained. No, she was not wet. Sam had driven her back to the office, to check that her story was okay, and waited to bring her back home. Did she want a drink? A cup of hot chocolate—she had been thinking longingly of that. Henry went to the kitchen to fix it for her, telling her to get warm by the heater.

"Good story?" he asked from the kitchen. "Where did you go?"

"Little village in Sussex, near Battle," she replied from the bedroom where she was stripping off her suit and getting into a housecoat. "Tell you about it when I've had my chocolate."

He brought it into the living-room. She sat by the heater drinking it. "Oh, how comforting. Thank you, darling. Yes, one hell of a good story. It'll lead page one, bound to."

Settling back into his own chair, Henry prompted, "So you went to a little village in Sussex, near Battle . . ."

Kate put down her cup and started to tell him all about it. Henry knew of the suit that Cornelius Ball had filed in the New York courts, it had been on the radio news. So then, Kate told him, remembering that Ursula Ball's great friend had been Angela Hughes, she had foxed up an interview with the actress. Henry whistled softly as she related briefly what she had learned.

"But that's not all, darling. I followed a hunch that Angela might be looking after Ursula's baby. So I conned the address of her country cottage out of the theatre publicity man, and that was the journey to the village near Battle. Not only was baby Cedric there with his nanny, but so was Cornelius Ball."

"Good story indeed!"

So then she had to tell him what she had learned from the American.

"I'm not revealing where the baby's hidden," she added, "and I'm not bringing Angela into it. I want my sources to myself. But I have reported that Cornelius was in England, stopping off to see his infant nephew, on a journey to the Middle East."

"Why is he going? Did you get that out of him?"

"To see the silversmith, of course, hoping to grab that 1954 penny before any other collector gets to him."

"Now I'm not only fascinated," Henry told her, "but quite lost."

"Oh, I forgot. You don't know about my service message from Geoff Wilton in Beirut. Seems that Cabral had a convenient sort of bank there—moved now to Damascus —and this silversmith, who obviously acted as his agent to sell rare coins on the world millionaire market. And the courier, who must have been carrying the coins for Cabral, was none other than Fred Sharp."

"The servant?"

"Exactly. So I trotted off to the basement of Cabral's house and pinned Fred down. One astonishing thing he admitted was that the job he came to London to do for Cabral that evening was to break in somewhere and steal something. He's an old hand at burglary; I gathered that Cabral took him on as an ex-convict. Fred didn't know where or what he was to burgle. My guess is Angela Hughes's flat in Knightsbridge, and the damning evidence with which she and George Roseveare intended to buy off Cabral."

"But the courier trips to Beirut?"

"Fred wouldn't admit anything. But I now feel fairly sure that the reason those three coins Cabral filched from Rosemary Ward were not in his 'small change' collection is that he had sent Fred Sharp off with them to the silversmith, to sell for huge sums, secretly and privately."

Henry was doubtful. "Why should he sell them? Cabral was very rich, and a fanatical numismatist. Those three coins would have completed his earthly paradise. So why should he sell?"

"Don't know," Kate admitted. "But I'm convinced that he sent them to be sold, and that Cornelius Ball had learned from the coin collectors' CIA that Hakim has at least one of them, probably the 1954 penny."

"Hakim?" asked Henry, startled. "Who's he?"

"The silversmith, Cabral's agent. Fouad Hakim. Cornelius tried to warn me off mentioning Hakim, saying that could be dangerous. What he was really trying to do, of course, was to ensure that no other coin expert, seeing Hakim named in my Cabral story, might catch on, make the right deductions, and either get there first or up the price. Very suave and very devious, his ex-excellency."

Henry got up to pour a Scotch. "Want one?"

"Not on top of hot chocolate, darling."

"I've an odd piece of news for you." He settled back in his chair with his glass. "An old woman called here this evening, wanting to see you. She was uttering a gipsy's warning, too. Very worried, I gathered, about what might happen to you, and what her grandson might get involved in, unless you dropped the Cabral investigation. Her grandson, she said, is a wild boy and will do what certain unidentified angry people tell him to do. She said she was a Mrs. Hakim, from Beirut."

*　　　*　　　*

Kate said, "I think perhaps I'll have a Scotch after all. She must be the woman who phoned me at the office and told me to lay off. Rather an odd, twisted accent?"

"You could call it that."

"Thanks," she said, taking the glass. "I thought she was just the usual newspaper-bothering crank. But then she rang the office the morning after I got mugged, and left a message to say she had warned me. So it looks as though the young fellow who knocked me down was Mrs. Hakim's grandson. And I'll confirm her view. He's wild."

"We must go to the police."

"With what? We don't really know anything."

"Then you must get Butch to put someone else on the story. If it involves that sort of risk, you've got to drop it."

"Hand this story over to somebody else? Not much! And don't bother about risk. All I have to do is watch it, not go down any dark alleys alone and that sort of thing. Never mind about that. What intrigues me is, why?"

She sipped her whisky. "I say, it does taste rather odd after hot chocolate. Still . . . Now, Henry, why should any-one want to stop me probing into the background to Cabral's death if he committed suicide?"

"There could be lots of reasons. Dubious business going on, for instance, that Cabral's death doesn't halt, that must remain under cover."

"Anyone can pull all sorts of reasons out of the air," replied Kate. "But the one that seems most likely is that Cabral did not commit suicide, but was murdered, and the murderer fears that, if I go on nosing around, I might be able to show that."

Henry spoke in his patience voice. "Darling, it just won't do. The burglar alarm."

"There could be another set of keys."

"Now listen. Detective Chief Inspector Aloysius Comfort is a very thorough man. My father speaks most highly of him. Bill Comfort, as he prefers to be called . . ."

"Understandably."

"Bill Comfort," went on Henry, ignoring the interruption, "would certainly not close any investigation until he had exhausted all possibilities and was convinced that he knew the truth.

"He is quite sure that there is not another set of keys and that the burglar alarm in Cabral's house is foolproof. I myself questioned him about it. He said that the finest electronics expert at Scotland Yard had examined the circuits and was certain that even the cleverest criminal—and they're dab hands these days at electronics—could not get into or out of that house without setting off the alarm, once the perimeter circuit was switched on.

"The highly reputable company that installed and maintained the system had, of course, no keys. Installation companies always hand all keys over to the householder. Nobody could have had an extra set of keys cut without producing the originals, and providing a written order signed by Cabral himself. Nobody ever did. The only set of keys, other than those held by Cabral himself and which were in his trousers pocket when we found his body, had never until then been removed from a strongbox in the strongroom of a keyholding company highly approved by Scotland Yard and simply, says Bill Comfort, above suspicion. It's just not on, Kate. Cabral shot himself."

Kate held out her glass. "Just a small one, please. If hot chocolate and whisky are an acquired taste, I think I could acquire it. Now then, let's forget all about that burglar alarm, and all those difficulties and, for the sake of argument, assume that Miles Cabral was murdered. Let's go over what we know. I'll recite it, and you take notes. Plenty of soda, please. Thanks."

Henry patiently fetched a pad of paper and a ballpoint from his desk.

"All right. Motive first. Who had motive?" he asked.

"Number one, George Roseveare, helped by Angela Hughes. Miles Cabral was about to bankrupt Roseveare and possibly lay him open, for all Angela's denial, to a criminal charge. There's this story that Angela is promoting, that George had enough on Cabral to blackmail him, and there's certainly evidence of something of that kind. But shooting him would be surer."

"Noted," said Henry.

"Number two, Jonathan Parr, hating Cabral for seducing his delectable girl-friend Rosemary, and then cheating her of three coins from the collection her uncle left her, she having no idea of their immense value."

"But would Jonathan have known their value either?"

"Why not? When I met them, he pretended to be suspicious but ignorant. But surely he could have checked Uncle's notebook list with an expert, or even looked coins up in a numismatic reference book in his public library."

"Possible," agreed Henry. "Very well."

"Number three, Cornelius Ball. There were moments when I felt that his hatred for Cabral, for what he had done to his sister Ursula, was almost demented. And Henry, come to think of it, those three with motive are all connected. George is living with Angela, who is a dear friend of Cornelius and is looking after Ursula's baby for him. Jonathan Parr is in the same play as Angela, and Rosemary, with whom he's living, is working as something or other in the same theatre. Can that be just coincidence?"

Henry smiled. "Teamwork, you think?"

"Could be," replied Kate uncertainly. "And Jonathan, of course, had an extra motive. If he shot Cabral in his coin room, he could have expected to take back the three coins the man cheated Rosemary out of."

"If he could find them," objected Henry. "I doubt if anyone except a coins expert could have picked out the right place to look for them in that very large collection, in what would have been a very limited time."

Kate agreed. "And anyway I don't think the coins were there. I'm pretty sure that Cabral had sent Fred Sharp off with them to Hakim the silversmith. But Jonathan would not have known that."

"Does that give Fred Sharp a motive?" suggested Henry. "Suppose he knew the great value of those coins. Suppose he and Fouad Hakim had decided to cheat Cabral and keep the coins for themselves, provided that Fred returned to London and got rid of his employer."

"Certainly possible," mused Kate. "Though I had the impression that Fred was deeply moved when he was shown Cabral lying on the floor. It could have been acting, but if so, rather good acting. And then it was Fred who started me off into investigating, by telling me of Mr. Grogan, the unblinking private eye. Still, I reckon we must grant that Fred could have had a motive."

"That brings us to Hakim the silversmith," said Henry, "and all this odd business of the terrified old woman, presumably his mother, and the wild boy, presumably his son. Hakim could have had the same motive as I suggested for Fred Sharp. Tempted by their unusual value, he intended to sell those coins for himself, which would mean killing Cabral before he found out. So the wild boy is sent to London to do the job. Cabral would certainly have known him and might well have let him into the house. So I'll add Fred Sharp and the Hakim family to the list."

"Ignoring the burglar alarm difficulty," said Kate, "what do we know of what went on that day around Cabral after we left him at the coin auction? Keep on taking notes, Henry. Cornelius said that he spoke to Cabral after the sale, and was asked to drinks that evening. We've only his word for it, and it seems unlikely."

"But he did go to the house."

"Stick to a timetable, Henry. We'll come to that later. Next, Cabral went to his club for lunch. While he was there, Angela Hughes, his ex-wife, threatened him by phone with some sort of exposure with material obtained from Cornelius Ball, unless he refrained from bankrupting George Roseveare, whom she's living with. Okay, said Cabral, come to the house at four o'clock and we'll talk."

"Is that the next item?"

"No. Immediately after Angela's phone call, Cabral phoned his own house in Sussex and told Fred Sharp to come to London that evening and bring his tools for house-breaking. The next thing we know is that Angela and George got to the house at four o'clock. Cabral wasn't there. But they waited, and he arrived in his car ten minutes later, took them in, they had their talk and they left at half past four."

"Authority for that being what Angela Hughes said at the inquest," noted Henry. "You didn't ask her about it?"

"No. Wish I had. But we got on to the Ursula story, and she broke off the interview when she let slip a remark that almost certainly meant that Cornelius Ball was lying in his affidavit to the coroner's court. She said that he threatened Miles that day with what was coming to him, and drove him to kill himself. I asked her if she meant that Cornelius had actually gone into the house, and she realized what she had said and threw me out."

"It doesn't necessarily mean that Ball was in the house," Henry argued. "He might have threatened Cabral by phone, or just possibly when they spoke after the auction in the sale room. But I admit the likeliest meaning is that he went there and Cabral let him in. He said he got there at five-thirty. But if he was lying about getting in, he could equally have been lying about time. So the only real fact we have in our timetable, that we can be sure of, is that

we arrived at eight minutes past six, and by then Cabral
was dead."

He handed over his notes.

"There you are, Kate. But it's an academic exercise.
Scotland Yard is satisfied that nobody except Cabral was
in that house from the time he died until our arrival.
Now let's go to bed. It's well past midnight."

CHAPTER 10

The coin fair was held in the banqueting chamber of a small, expensive hotel just off Piccadilly. Henry, half jokingly, had suggested to Kate that she should come along, since she had developed such a keen interest in numismatics.

What was a coin fair? Leading dealers from the big cities hired booths and sold their coins, chiefly to one another, though some to private collectors and a few to members of the public who had wandered in out of curiosity. There were perhaps a dozen coin fairs during the course of a year, most of them in London, but a few elsewhere; a particularly notable one in Manchester, another in Brighton. The fairs were specially useful to dealers from smaller towns; kept them in touch with the trade.

It was a top-market occasion, Kate saw at once. The booths were arrangements of small glass-topped show tables, a few chairs for clients, desks for the dealers and their secretaries, most of the girls evidently chosen more for their looks than their shorthand. The booths lined two sides of the discreetly opulent banqueting room. At the far end was a temporary cash bar, covered in fine white linen, served by three hotel barmen. The bar was busy, although it was scarcely half past ten in the morning. Champagne by the glass seemed to be the numismatists' favourite tipple.

The long room was brilliantly lit—no vulgarity of windows, of course—and humming with chatter. All the exhibitors and their customers seemed to know each other, so that it was rather a jolly family gathering, a day-off enjoyment. Henry, she noted approvingly, was one of them. He greeted and was greeted several times as they walked in.

"There's Arthur Toogood," he told her, making for a booth half-way along the room. "I must introduce you. He's a fountain of gossip. Everything going on, Arthur knows it. He's a great expert, and the best numismatics valuer in London. He has a little shop behind Albany. It's one of the oldest-established businesses. Arthur's father had it before him and, I believe, grandfather before that. Medieval and Renaissance European are Arthur's personal specialty, but his knowledge is superb over the whole range, from the earliest Lydian—the coins of Croesus himself—up to the modern rarities, particularly modern American. My father has bought a lot from him, and I a little. He also happens to be a member of my club. Arthur, may I introduce my wife?"

Arthur Toogood was a tall, burly man of early middle age with a broadly smiling manner, most amiable. He was enchanted to meet Mrs. Theobald, and my dear Henry they must of course have a drink together. So they made for the bar, Arthur chattering jollily of what was new and what was amusing, and what he could put Henry on to, in particular some good early-American. One of his oldest customers had recently died, and the heir was not interested in coins. So Arthur was disposing of a really rather good early-American collection, a line in which he knew Henry was specially interested, at really rather bargain prices. Henry, laughing, begged him not to mention, in his wife's hearing, the actual sums he was to be tempted to spend. Whacko, Arthur agreed, handing them glasses of champagne. Kate began to think she was going to enjoy a coin fair after all, though without in the least understanding what they were all talking about. It was rather like being at an agreeable drinks party in a foreign country.

Arthur turned to her to say, "By the way, Mrs. Theobald, you'll be interested to know that I've been spending days in that room where you found Miles Cabral's body." He laughed. "Oh, nothing dramatic. Not a newspaper story. I've simply been hired by his lawyers to value the coin collection for probate."

"Must be an immense sum," said Henry.

"I'll say! I've valued a few in my time, as you know, Henry. But Cabral's is ahead of most of them."

"How do you get into the house?" asked Kate.

Arthur chuckled. "It's a hell of a business. Scotland

Yard sends a police car to my shop each morning—the neighbours are beginning to look at me very strangely. In the car there's a Detective Sergeant Chin. Splendid chap, very friendly. We're on drinking terms now—have a couple of pints together at the nearest pub after every session in the house. Chin says it's one of the strongest reasons for being a plain-clothes policeman, you can drink in pubs."

"So he has keys to the house?"

"Oh yes, to the house and to the burglar alarm, or part of it anyhow. Seems there's a double circuit, but the police are keeping only the perimeter switched on." Arthur laughed again. "You'd not credit the reason for that. To switch on the inner circuit, they'd have to break open a wall safe in the hall, where its control panel is. It's a combination lock, and only poor old Miles himself knew the combination. He had switched it off—the valuables circuit he called it—that afternoon when he shot himself, to get into the coins room to get his revolver. So it was out of action when he died, and has stayed that way ever since. Chin says it doesn't seem worth having the wall safe broken open, now there's nobody living there. Any intruder's bound to spark off the perimeter alarm, and that's all that's needed.

"Great fuss they make at the Yard about the keys to that, Chin tells me. He has to register them in and out, and they're kept in some very well-guarded place when he turns them in."

"How about valuation of all the other treasures?" asked Henry.

"Chin took along men from Sotheby's. I don't know the figure, but I reckon the pictures and furniture could be worth even more than the coins. But that's all been done. There's only the coin collection now, and I've nearly finished. Another session or two and I'll have the total. Staggering, it'll be, Henry."

Kate asked, "Will the police then take anybody else in—cleaners or anybody—or will it then stay locked?"

"It'll stay locked, Chin says. They asked Miles's lawyers, but they said just to keep it locked. So now they've put one of their own locks on the door of the cupboard where the alarm control is, and Chin says that, when I've finished, they'll seal it up." Arthur's laugh guffawed again. "Damn funny. The lawyers were going to send everything for auction, once the valuations were done. But some joker's making a claim on the estate, and his lawyers are insisting that everything must be frozen pending court hearings. It's giving Miles's lot high blood pressure! When they told me, I said they'd better get somebody in to check my valuation list against the coins themselves. Matter of fact, I insisted on it. So Wilf Spooner came in yesterday, to go over my earlier list while I went on with the cabinets I still hadn't valued. You know Wilf, of course, Henry. Reliable chap."

"Second best in London."

Arthur laughed loudly and patted him on the back. "Well done, Henry. The *mot juste*. But do you know what, I'm damn glad I did insist on an independent check. Wilf found a couple of mistakes I'd made. It's a fact. First time it's happened to me in years—or ever, I could say. I'd listed a couple of coins that weren't there. Hot ones too. Must have confused them with another couple. The old brain's giving out," he declared. "Getting on for time they put me out. Luckily my boy's nearly ready to come into the business."

"Is Gregory still at Oxford?" asked Henry.

"No, he came down a year ago. Since then I've been sending him round museums, working with the staffs. He's just finished a stint in Germany and gone off to Switzerland. After that, he's going to the States for a few months. Then he'll come back to London and join me in the shop. Better hand it over to him, eh? before I get completely decrepit."

Kate saw Henry nod and smile to a man who was coming towards the bar, and whose somewhat sallow face she seemed vaguely to remember, though she could not place him. She murmured to Henry, who was that, did she know him?

"It's Harvey Foskett. You remember? He bought that Charles crown."

"Oh, of course.'

Foskett came up to them. "The *young* Mr. Theobald," he said, smiling at the recalled joke. "Is your father here?"

"The young and still impoverished Mr. Theobald," replied Henry. "No, my father has to be in court all day, alas. But may I introduce my wife?"

Harvey Foskett bowed slightly and said it was a pleasure. "I've seen you before, Mr. Foskett," she said, "at that auction where you bought a Charles I crown, for an unnamed client who was emphatically not Miles Cabral."

Foskett smiled his wintry smile. "Thank you. I am glad indeed that that is firmly established."

"Have you sold it yet?" asked Henry.

"A glass of champagne, Harvey?" enquired Arthur Toogood.

"Why, thank you, Arthur." To Henry he said solemnly, "Since I bought it for that anonymous client, Mr. Theobald, it could not have been mine, exactly, to sell, eh?" He allowed himself a little smirk. "But, between ourselves—well, I no longer have it."

"I read what you wrote in the *Post* about Cabral and the 1954 penny, Mrs. Theobald," said Arthur. "It sounded very romantic. Journalistic licence, eh?"

"Do call me Kate. And I admit I did perhaps allow a little imagination, as it were, to play upon the actual facts."

Arthur chortled at that. "But I'll not give you away."

"So that's why you come to ask me about the 1954 penny, is it, Mr. Theobald?" asked Foskett, faintly amused. "You were not really intending to sell me that 1738 two-guinea piece?"

"I asked Henry to make a few enquiries from the most knowledgeable person he knew, Mr. Foskett," replied Kate. "Like an excellent husband, he did his best to oblige me, just as I'm sure you always do what Mrs. Foskett asks."

"An old bachelor, I'm sorry to say, Mrs. Theobald. But not unappreciative of Mr. Theobald's husbandly obedience."

"I can give you an amusing story about the 1954 penny for your paper, if you like, Kate," Arthur Toogood interrupted. "A young fellow came to my shop with a scribbled list of a few coins, and asked me if any of them was valuable. Whoever gave him the list had been having him on. It must have been some sort of bet, or a quiz at a party, or something like that. Most of the coins listed were ordinary rubbish, but there were three I'll defy any of you to guess."

"Don't keep us in suspense," urged Henry.

"Okay. A 1954 penny, a 1933 penny and a Teddy VIII threepenny bit. So I told him, if he brought any one of those to me, be careful not to handle or mark it, and I'd pay him enough to retire on; bring all three, and he could have his own Greek island."

Arthur laughed happily at the absurdity of it.

"Not your usual cautious buying talk, Arthur," said Henry.

"I wasn't really anticipating a purchase, old boy. '54 and '33 pennies and a Teddy VIII threepenny. Can you beat it? Some young actor, he said he was. I don't remember his name. I wondered if some joker had challenged him to try to take the micky out of me."

"Did you ever see him again?" asked Kate innocently.

"Bless you, no. Not a smell of him. Ah, I get it. You're trying for a follow-up to your article about Miles, and maybe he had that coin. Sorry to disappoint you."

"Curiously, though," put in Foskett, "there is some sort of rumour going round, with what strength I simply don't know, that a 1954 penny is on offer."

"I heard that one too," agreed Arthur. "Several of us did. But it's a perennial, ain't it? There's never anything in it. The suggestion is that whoever bought that specimen that was sold a few years ago in the States has put it back on the closed-circuit market. But I think I know who did buy it, as I expect you do too, Harvey. Yes, I thought so. And we both know that that gentleman isn't selling anything, and never will while he lives. And this time there's an extra absurdity. One chap I got it from said there was supposed to be a 1933 penny as well."

"I hadn't heard that," said Foskett. "Now, let me replenish your glasses. Oh yes please, I insist."

"Maybe," said Arthur Toogood, laughing at the idea, "it was that young actor fellow keeping his joke going."

In the taxi on the way to their weekly lunch at Henry's club, Kate said suddenly, "Do you think it likely that your jovial friend Arthur, the finest numismatic valuer in London, working on a collection that obviously excited him, can really have absent-mindedly listed two coins that were not there?"

She had been pondering this while she hung about in the coin fair, waiting as Henry wandered from one booth to another, and eventually bought something from Arthur Toogood for, Kate felt sure, a price he could not really afford. For if the Homer of the coin world had not in fact nodded, the implication could be significant. If those two coins had been in their little nests in the cabinet on the day that Arthur listed them, and were not there a few days later when Wilf came to check, what had happened to them?

"I suppose he might have," Henry replied, "though I would not have believed it if he hadn't told us himself."

"There could be another explanation—that they were there when Arthur valued them, and later somebody took them."

"Took them? But who? The furniture and picture valuers had done their work and gone. There was nobody else in the house except Sergeant Chin. Surely you don't think . . ."

"Chin the incorruptible? No, of course I don't. Aside from anything else, he would not have known which coins were most worth snitching. Arthur himself would have known, of course . . ."

"Oh, come now, Kate."

"A member of your club! All right, I'm not suggesting that. So what alternatives are there? Either Arthur made an untypical mistake in his professional capacity, or somebody who knows about coins got into the house later, when it was supposed to be locked by that unbreakable burglar alarm."

"The intruder would have to have keys."

"Exactly, Henry. Do please stop dreaming about that coin you bought this morning, and apply your brilliant legal mind to what I am saying. Unless Arthur boobed, there must be another set of keys, at least to the front door and the perimeter-alarm control panel. If someone could get in there now, he could equally have got out, and reset the alarm, after shooting Miles Cabral."

Henry shifted uneasily on the taxi seat. Well, she demanded, what other deduction could there be?

"Arthur boobed, of course."

"Henry, I want you to go and see that Scotland Yard man. Tell him what we heard this morning. Ask him if he doesn't think that he should check and check again on the possibility of another set of keys existing—and if so, who could have them?"

Henry reluctantly agreed. "But I'll probably get only a polite request to let the police go about their business in their own way."

Detective Chief Inspector Comfort was readier to listen than Henry had expected. He agreed at once to a telephoned request for a meeting, and when Henry got to his office in the tower block at New Scotland Yard, and told him of Arthur Toogood's remark, Comfort was all attention.

"I know that Mrs. Theobald has never been convinced that Cabral shot himself," he said slowly, thoughtfully, "and from what I have read in her newspaper, she has been trying to find some evidence to the contrary."

"Her job as a reporter . . ." put in Henry apologetically.

"Don't think that our minds are closed. An inquest verdict, as you know as a lawyer, isn't necessarily the end of everything. We are indeed still concerned with that house, because we have to keep strict control of it until the valuables are all listed and so on. If it could be shown that another set of keys exists, then of course the whole matter would look very different and our enquiries would be reopened.

"Now, sir, Mr. Toogood is an old friend of yours. You know him well as a coin expert. Tell me what you think. Did Mr. Toogood make that mistake?"

"I don't know what to say, Mr. Comfort. In any other circumstances I should have found it incredible that he could have done so. But if that implies the existence of another set of keys to Cabral's house . . ."

"Let me tell you briefly, sir, what our enquiries produced," offered the policeman. "The first consideration was that Mr. Cabral himself had a set of keys cut for somebody else—for his wife, say. But, as Miss Hughes stated at the inquest, the alarm systems, we found, were installed after she and Cabral had divorced.

"He might have given keys to one of his mistresses." Comfort smiled gently. "I understand that, from time to time, there were quite a few young ladies who would qualify. If so, he would have to have gone to the burglar-alarm company, signed a written request that would have been entered into a special book, and later signed a receipt for a set of keys. He never did.

"I suppose he could have taken his set of keys to some underground, criminal locksmith. But why should he, when he could perfectly easily have new keys cut legally? But we didn't accept that without enquiring among the very few criminal locksmiths in the country. We know them all, of course. Negative. Not only negative that Cabral himself had a set cut, but that anybody else did. And, of course, nobody else could have done so without having in his possession the master set which Cabral kept always on his person."

"How about the emergency keys?"

"Admitted. There has to be an emergency set to let the police cope if the alarm should be triggered accidentally when Cabral himself was out of the country, as he often was.

"We advised him about this when the circuits were installed. On our advice, he lodged the emergency keys with a key-holding company which has close connections with the Yard, and which we trust implicitly. But for premises which have unusually valuable contents we insist that the keys are kept in a strongbox that requires two keys to open it, one held by the Yard, one by the company.

"When you and Mrs. Theobald triggered the alarm, a senior police officer was sent with our strongbox key to the company's premises, and he collected the emergency keys to Cabral's house.

"I don't have to tell you, Mr. Theobald, that nothing is absolutely watertight, and we are all prone to human error. But those arrangements convince me, anyhow, that there are no other keys in existence, except the emergency keys and the set we found in Cabral's trousers pocket.

"Since that night, we have held both sets and, as I said, a very tight control is kept on them. Satisfied, Mr. Theobald?"

"How can I not be?"

"And you'll recount all this to Mrs. Theobald? Off the record, of course, not for newspaper publication. I hope she also will be satisfied."

"I'll tell her," agreed Henry, "strictly off the record." He smiled. "But I can't guarantee that she will be satisfied. After all, women . . ."

CHAPTER 11

When Kate returned to the office that afternoon, the news-desk secretary asked her to call Larry Corcoran, the theatre publicity man. He had been through three times trying to reach her. Kate said to raise him and switch him through.

"Hallo, Larry. Sorry about that interview. But Angela Hughes changed her mind and asked me to drop it."

"I know. She told me. Heaven knows why. Theatre publicity would be a lovely job, if I didn't have to deal with actresses. And actors. Kate, I'm damn sorry you were put to all that trouble for nothing."

"Sometimes you win, sometimes you lose."

"What I hope is that it may not be wasted—if you would do me a great favour."

"Which is?"

"See her again."

"But she refused."

"I've been talking to her and I think she could be persuaded, if you went to her again. I know it's one hell of a thing to ask a newspaperwoman of your standing. If she doesn't want the publicity, sod her. But it isn't bloody Angela Hughes I'm thinking about. It's the rest of the company. Fact is, the play's going to close tomorrow night, which means a dozen nice people out of work and very little chance of getting anything else for months. But there's just a chance that a tour can be fixed up, which would keep them working for a few more weeks anyway, perhaps longer. The agent we're tackling is a bit doubtful, but he hasn't actually turned down the idea. A really good bit of publicity might tip the balance. I'm ashamed to be asking you this, after the way that bloody woman behaved. But . . ."

"I never stand on my dignity, Larry. Not much dignity

to stand on. All right, if Angela will agree. But it must be clear that any piece I write will be about her, because the Cabral story isn't dead, and looks like hotting up into legal battles."

"But you'll mention the play?"

"Sure. I'll work in a bit of a plug if you like. When do I go to see Miss Hughes?"

"Call you back in ten minutes."

When he came through again, he said, "She's being damn difficult. But I tell you what. There's a closing party on the stage after the last performance tomorrow night. Would you come along?"

"Won't that be a little late, after the play has closed? I couldn't get it into the paper until two mornings later. They wouldn't take that sort of piece in late editions."

"It's the chance of a tour I'm thinking of, Kate. If I could tell the agent that there might be a good piece by you in the *Post*, that'd probably clinch it."

"Suppose she still won't agree?"

"I think she will," he said, "if you're actually there, asking her. And I'll get at her and stress the point that it's for the sake of the others."

"All right, Larry. I take it I may bring my husband. Good. We'll attend the obsequies."

"It'll be a jolly party," he assured her. "Stage parties after the first night are often gloomy, but not after the last performance. By then, everybody's getting sloshed, and optimistic about the next job, and couldn't care less anyhow. Thanks a lot, Kate. Quarter past eleven at the stage door. Or would you like to see the play first?"

"Don't push your luck, Larry."

So Henry took her for a leisurely supper to that small place in Dean Street where they knew him and always kept the table in the window for him. Afterwards they walked round to the stage door. It was a dark, cold night, but not raining.

Billy in his hutch was transformed. He had actually taken off his bowler hat and was smoking a cigar. He took a sip from a large whisky in a thick tumbler, and told them, "Mr. Corcoran says you're to go right in."

There was no difficulty in finding the way to the stage. The noise was already boisterous. They stood for a few minutes in the shelter of the wings, looking around. The safety curtain was down, the scenery for the last act had not been shifted. Must have been the drawing-room of Sir Somebody's country house in Sussex, Kate thought, with wide french windows opening to a tawdrily-painted garden backcloth. Near to, in this garish lighting, everything looked used-up and dusty.

But not the people—actors, stage hands, front-of-the-house-staff, everybody, even Billy who, having now been able to close the stage door, came happily in with his glass and cigar. Most of them were gathered round a bare trestle table at the back of the stage supporting plates of thick sandwiches, sausage rolls, wedges of pork pie and a splendid collection of bottles and glasses. The din was rowdy. Already a couple of the younger girls were laughing at an alcoholically high pitch. The older men, more experienced in adversity, were concentrating on the sandwiches.

"Look at that marvellous brunette standing to the right of the table," Henry murmured admiringly.

"She," said Kate severely, "is Rosemary Ward, the girl Miles Cabral set up in that love-nest in Kensington in order to snitch her uncle's coins."

"Fancy needing a motive."

"And I should warn you, Henry, that the tall, very handsome young man beside her, who is a good deal younger and probably more muscular than you, is Jonathan Parr, her boy-friend."

"Pity."

Larry Corcoran came hastening across the stage. "Good of you to come, Kate. Is this Mr. Theobald? Hallo, then. Let me get you drinks. Scotch? Come on in properly."

As they stood near the table and Larry fetched the drinks, Kate saw Jonathan Parr spot her, look startled, then turn his back as though he had not noticed, to talk to a man beside him. Rosemary did not seem to recognize her. Angela Hughes, as leading lady, was surrounded by a small group, all joking merrily and swallowing hard.

Larry, seeing Kate's glance, promised, "I'll detach her in a few minutes and bring her to you. Over in the wings, away from the crowd?"

Kate nodded.

So after a while he drifted across to say something to Angela Hughes, and then led her back to them.

"Let's leave the women to talk," he said to Henry, "and go get us another drink."

"I had a phone call from Cornelius," said Angela.

"From Beirut?"

"From Damascus, actually. He said I should be grateful to you for not revealing where Cedric is hidden and for keeping me out of it. So I'm grateful."

"Then show it by agreeing to our interview. I've promised Larry that, if you do, I'll put a piece in the paper. He thinks it would get a tour fixed and keep all these others in work for a while longer."

"What do you want to write?"

"Probably be a couple of paragraphs in the diary. Meet-you here, I think, and a few words from you about carrying on with your career in spite of. Something like that. I'll plug the play. Larry thinks it could do the trick."

"All right. Now I've been grateful, like Cornelius said. Now tell me. How did you find out about Cedric being there?"

Kate felt smug. "Nose for news. I just played a hunch that, because of your closeness to Ursula, he might be. Nobody else has found out, have they? No reporters been round that cottage?"

"No. And I've warned Mrs. Horton to be absolutely careful not to give anything away. I had to, because she would have seen your article in the *Post* and might have said something locally, not thinking. A good many reporters have been on to me, I don't know why."

"Just desperation. There's quite a fuss, among some of our rivals, at not being able to find the baby. So they're trying everybody who had any sort of connection with Miles or Cornelius. The London bureaux of the American papers are being pressured hardest by their offices."

"A couple of men who came to see me were American. They didn't get anything."

"Good for you."

After a pause, Angela said hesitantly, "I want some help."

"From me? Of course, if I can."

"George's divorce is now absolute, and I want to get married straight away. He won't until he has straightened out the financial mess he's in. He says it wouldn't be fair to me, which is rubbish. He thinks that newspaper influence might be useful in a deal he's trying to arrange. Will you talk to him?"

"Be happy to. But I'd better bring in my husband too.

He's a lawyer, and understands that sort of thing much better than I do."

Henry and Larry were coming back towards them.

"Henry, come and talk to Angela Hughes."

"Larry," said Angela, "be a dear and ask George to step over."

"Sure. Interview agreed? Oh, that's super."

When George Roseveare came over, Kate found herself liking him. A pleasant man. She asked how she could help.

"Well, I expect you know roughly the sort of mess I made of becoming a property millionaire. And Angela tells me you have guessed, or something, that Cabral had bought up most of my debts and was going to bankrupt me, because of her. Well, of course, his executors have the same idea—not anything to do with Angela, but to straighten up the estate. I've asked them if they would, instead, let me fund the debts—all short-term—with a long-term loan on the security of the properties."

"But surely," put in Henry, "your whole difficulty is that the properties, at present values, are nothing like sufficient security for the size of your bank borrowings."

"Exactly. But I have a certain amount of pressure I can put on the executors. Let's say that there are some aspects of Cabral's business affairs that they would prefer not to get known. So they've gone so far as to agree to negotiate a long-term loan, at reasonable rates, if I can get reputable City backing for a fairly substantial amount. Trouble is, with my track record, I can't. But the basic property situation is reasonably sound, if you take a fairly optimistic view. If I hadn't made such an ass of myself by borrowing wildly during the boom, I should have a modestly viable concern." To Henry he said, "I can give you all the figures."

"I've no influence in the City."

"But the *Post* has," said Kate. "If you really have got a reasonable position, I'll arrange for you to tell old Frank about it, in our City office. He'll know for sure if it can be done."

"That would be marvellous. May I send you the figures?"

Kate laughed. "Not unless they're in Chinese. My dear man, I can scarcely add up the housekeeping accounts. Ask Henry. Bet he would understand them. If you can convince Henry, then I'll approach old Frank. But not unless."

"Free for lunch tomorrow?" Henry asked him. "At my club?"

"Fine."

Kate turned to Angela. "Now, since we're talking of doing deals, and tit for tat and all that, will you please tell me something?"

"Depends."

"What seems odd to me is that Angela Hughes, Cabral's former wife, who was being threatened with disaster by him, should be in the same play as Jonathan Parr, who hated Cabral for taking Rosemary as his mistress and robbing her, he thinks, of rare coins worth a fortune. And Rosemary is working as an usherette or something in the same theatre. Just coincidence?"

"Not entirely. Jonathan came to me when Miles got hold of Rosemary, who's a lovely but rather simple child. I'm very fond of her. Jonathan knew me. We'd been together in a television play two years ago. He was seething. Wasn't there some way we could get at Miles?

"At that time I didn't think there was. But it happened that a young actor had dropped out of the cast—gone to the States—so I got Jonathan the job. He's good, you know. He'll get on.

"We both tried to think of something. Some short time later, when Miles threw Rosemary out and she went back to Jonathan, he got her a job here as an usherette. Always a shortage of them."

"And did you think of anything?" asked Kate.

"Cornelius thought of it for us."

"For you. But surely not for Jonathan."

"Well, I sort of included him and Rosemary in the threat to Miles that afternoon. He must give the girl back those coins."

"And he just laughed?"

"He was sneering about the whole thing. I see now that he felt pretty sure of getting his burglar to get hold of our evidence. It wouldn't really have done him all that much good. Cornelius promised plenty more ammunition if the first shot misfired."

"So you had to tell Jonathan you had failed to get the coins returned?"

"Yes. I rang him up straight away, at his digs, directly George and I got home to our flat after leaving Miles. The wretched boy was waiting by his phone for news."

"And you told him no go. What time would that be?"

Angela looked vague. "Oh, about a quarter to five, I suppose."

By asking Henry to get her another drink, then drifting away as he brought it back to her, Kate managed to get him alone, sufficiently out of earshot.

"I've felt all along, Henry, that it wasn't just coincidence that Angela, Jonathan and Rosemary were all in the same theatre, all hating Miles Cabral. At least, Rosemary didn't hate him, she's too nice to hate anybody, but of course she would have liked her uncle's coins back, once Jonathan told her how much Miles had got away with. Now, you heard what Angela just told me."

"So?"

"So what did Jonathan do when he got the phone call? That's what I'd like to know."

"You think that, in a rage, and knowing Cabral was at home, he stormed round there, and . . . and what?"

"I can see him getting into a cab and arriving, say, at about a quarter past five. It's not far from Clapham. He rings the bell, he gets his foot in the door, pushes his way in. No question, of course, of any interference from the burglar alarm. Cabral would have switched it off when he entered the house. That's normal with burglar alarms. When you're at home, you switch the thing off, so that you can go around, and in and out, without bothering about it. I had a talk with a friend of mine who has an alarm fitted. If you're at home, you don't switch it on until you go to bed at night."

"At the inquest," Henry reminded her, "Angela said she heard Cabral turn the alarm key in the lock in the front door after he had let her out."

Kate paused for a moment, remembering. "No, she didn't," she answered. "When the coroner asked her if Cabral had switched the alarm on after she left, she asked how could she know. It was the coroner who put it to her about hearing the key in the lock, and she simply agreed as the easiest way of finishing her spell of evidence. It was just one more lie on top of the others. She wouldn't risk a contradiction that might interest the coroner."

Henry conceded that. "Go on with your imaginative fiction about Jonathan. He has just pushed his way into the house. So what follows?"

"Jonathan sees the coins-room door open, and the cabinets inside. He threatens Cabral—give the coins back, or he'll knock him cold and take them. Cabral backs into the coins room, feels behind him into the drawer where he keeps his gun, but Jonathan sees him, there's a struggle, Jonathan grabs the gun, it goes off, accidentally perhaps."

"So then you think he took the coins? I doubt if he could have found them in less than a couple of hours, in that big collection, unless he knew how to set about it."

"That doesn't matter," argued Kate. "I don't think the coins were there anyway. I think Cabral had already sent Fred Sharp with them to Beirut. Seeing Cabral dead, Jonathan wouldn't have been thinking any longer about coins, anyhow, but simply how to get away."

"And how," asked Henry politely, "do you think he did that, setting the burglar alarm, of which he had no knowledge, behind him?"

"Henry, don't make difficulties. That burglar-alarm question has got to be answered some time, it must be. Because I'm now certain that Cabral didn't shoot himself. Aren't you?"

Henry raised his hands helplessly. "I have to admit that there were reasons . . . But that alarm system . . . I simply don't know."

She put her hand on his arm. "Good. You're starting to agree with me. Let's forget the damned alarm for a while, and see if we can discover what Jonathan did after he got that phone call from Angela."

"Just ask him, you mean?"

"Darling, you're a skilled advocate, accustomed by brilliant cross-examination to squeeze the truth out of even the most reluctant or artful witness."

Henry laughed. "Okay. I'll ask him. Take me over. The only condition is that I'm introduced to the brunette too."

Jonathan saw them coming and looked uneasy. Rosemary, by his side, did not seem to notice.

"Well, hallo," Kate said. "I'd like you to meet my husband. Jonathan Parr and Rosemary Ward."

Jonathan nodded. The girl looked blank.

"Remember me?" asked Kate. "I'm the one who didn't have a kipper for tea."

Rosemary broke into the most enchanting smile. "Oh, of course. The girl from the newspaper."

She's acting, Kate thought to herself; and she's not much of an actress.

For that sort of situation there is a classic interviewing technique. Jump straight in. It was evidently also a classic cross-examining technique, for it was Henry who jumped.

"We've just been having a chat with Miss Hughes. How interesting that you two went round to Miles Cabral's house that afternoon. Did he actually let you in?"

"Not into the house," said Rosemary, suddenly scared.

Kate was privately amused to notice how angry Jonathan was that she had walked so neatly into it. Henry would not have pulled it off with him alone.

The best he could do now, however, was to mutter that he wasn't going to discuss that with Henry. Absolutely nothing to say.

"Come on, Jonathan," urged Kate. "It's important. Can't you see how important it is for Angela and George? If it wasn't suicide—and the police are not at all sure that it was, in spite of the inquest verdict—then it's vital for Angela and George to be able to establish that somebody saw Miles after they had left him."

"Nothing to say."

But Rosemary broke in with, "Oh Johnny, if that's what they're thinking . . ."

She turned to Kate.

"It isn't so, what you're thinking about Angela. We saw Miles. No, Johnny, don't interrupt. After we got Angela's phone call to say that Miles had laughed at her, Johnny grabbed a taxi and we both went to the house. We paid off the taxi at the end of the little road. It was dark and gloomy down there, not much street lighting. As we walked towards the house, the front door opened and Miles came out with another man."

"What was the other man like?" asked Henry sharply.

"Couldn't see much of him. He had his coat collar up against the weather, and went off past us on the other side of the road. Besides, we weren't thinking about him. We both ran forward to get hold of Miles before he went in and shut his door."

"And did you?"

Jonathan evidently decided that, since Rosemary had admitted they were there, he would take charge.

"Yes, we did," he said. "He didn't go back into his house straight away. His Rolls was standing by the kerb. He walked over to get something out of it—a book I think. Then he saw me and Rosie."

"Did he dodge back?"

"Not a bit. He laughed, and said that he was having a busy afternoon, and what had I come to threaten him with? I said it wasn't a question of threats. I simply wanted him to give back to Rosie the three coins he had stolen from her uncle's collection."

"He denied it?" asked Henry.

"No. He was quite blatant about it. He said, 'Sure, I have those coins.' "

Kate asked, "Did he say 'I have them' or 'I had them'?"

Jonathan thought. "I'm fairly sure he said 'I have those coins.' Does it matter?"

"It might."

She said no more. Jonathan had obviously not seen the significance—that it could mean the coins were in his coins room that afternoon. Though she had to admit to herself that it was a weak deduction.

Jonathan shrugged. "Well, I think that's the way he put it. Then he said he had brought them quite legally. Rosemary had given him the collection to sell, and he himself had bought it for fifty-two pounds. He had asked her if she accepted that price, and she had, and had signed a receipt for the cash."

"Did you?" asked Kate.

Rosemary admitted it. "I never thought . . ."

"Of course you didn't," Kate soothed her. "Why should you?"

Jonathan went on. "Then he had the gall to smirk and say, 'I'm a business man. I buy in the cheapest market and sell in the dearest.' I could have hit him."

"The police might wonder whether you did," murmured Henry.

Rosemary was indignant. "But he didn't. I can bear witness to that."

"I wonder how much that would count for?"

Now the girl was suddenly scared again. "The police? Why the police?"

Jonathan answered her. "What Mr. Theobald is hinting is that the police might suspect that I had one hell of a row with Miles—which would be for the second time—and followed him into his house, and shot him with his own gun."

"But that's not true," Rosemary insisted, wide-eyed. What a wonderfully pretty girl she was, Kate thought. "Miles just sneered at us, and told Johnny to do what he liked about it. And he said, whatever he did, he promised not to sue him for slander. He was absolutely horrid."

Jonathan smiled. "Better shut up, darling, you're making it worse. Mr. Theobald can practically see me in the dock at the Old Bailey already."

"Don't worry," Henry assured him. "If they charged you, I'd defend you myself. Because you have a perfect answer to the charge. Whether you went into the house or not, you did not shoot Cabral and come out again. Not unless you had keys to the burglar alarm. But just for the defence's information, did you go into the house?"

Sobered, Jonathan told him, "No. There was nothing I could do. I realized that. The bastard had those coins and we'd never get them back. I had to stand there while he walked back into the house and shut the door. Then Rosemary and I came away."

"It would also help the defence if there happened to be anybody around who could substantiate what you say."

"There was that man coming down the street, Johnny," Rosemary reminded him.

"That was after Miles had gone into the house and we were coming away."

"Oh yes," she recalled. "So it was."

Kate asked, "This man who came down the street and must have passed you—it's a cul-de-sac, isn't it? Where did he go?"

"Into one of the houses," said Rosemary. "I glanced back when we got to the corner."

"Mile's house?"

Rosemary looked doubtful. "It might have been. It was on that side of the road. But I'm not sure."

"What was the man like—tall or short, fat or thin?"

"About average," said Jonathan.

"On the tall side," said Rosemary. "I think he was carrying something in his left hand." She paused. "Yes, left hand."

"What sort of thing?"

"Oh, a briefcase, I think. Something like that. Look, you're not really going to tell the police, are you?"

Henry looked at Jonathan. "It would be sensible for you to go to the police yourself and tell them what you have told us. You've absolutely nothing to fear, except probably a ticking-off for not coming forward earlier. If I were you, tomorrow morning, first thing. I'd telephone Detective Chief Inspector Comfort at Scotland Yard and arrange to go along and see him."

"Oh Johnny, perhaps you should," whispered Rosemary, talking hold of his hand. "I'll come with you."

Jonathan said nothing.

When a little later the Theobalds left the party, nodding to Larry Corcoran, Billy (now a bit wobbly) unlocking the stage door for them, Kate asked Henry, "Do you think he will?"

"I think so. But whether he does or not, we must. I'll ring Comfort from my chambers tomorrow."

He hailed a taxi. As they got in, Kate told the driver, "*Daily Post* office."

Henry looked a protest.

"My darling Henry, you don't think I'm going to pass that story up, do you? I'll make the late editions. You'll have to sit around while I write it."

He looked unhappy. "Do be careful, Kate. What are you going to say?"

"I won't name those two youngsters—not yet, anyway. The story will be that new evidence has come up. A man was seen leaving Cabral's house at about a quarter past five that afternoon. Cabral himself came into the street and had an argument with another man and a young woman who were coming to see him, but whom he would not let into his house. But they saw another man who rang Cabral's doorbell and was admitted to the house by Cabral himself a few minutes later. The police have now re-opened their enquiries."

"You can't be sure of that."

"It's a fair guess, Henry." She giggled. "You won't need to go to Chief Inspector Comfort tomorrow. He'll come to us."

CHAPTER 12

As indeed he did. The Chief Inspector telephoned the Theobalds' flat at eight next morning, while they were having breakfast.

He was there within fifteen minutes of ensuring that they were at home. Sergeant Chin climbed the stairs with him. Henry was amused to see that Comfort was puffing a little.

"Sorry about all those stairs, Mr. Comfort. It's why the flat is cheap enough for us to afford."

Kate emerged from the kitchen with a tray. "Coffee? I've kept it warm."

When they were settled in the living-room she said, "I suppose it's because of my piece in the *Post* this morning."

"Partly," said Comfort.

Chin took a copy of that morning's edition from his briefcase and handed it to him.

"What you have written about the two men said to have been seen by a young couple as they left and entered Cabral's house, and about Cabral's argument with the couple—I take it you got the information from either the young man or the young woman."

"Mr. Comfort, you must know that a newspaper reporter never reveals sources."

Comfort regarded her gravely. "Mrs. Theobald, you have a responsibility as a citizen. Withholding evidence from the police can be a very serious matter. I'm sure your husband, as a lawyer, will confirm that."

"Of course withholding evidence that might help the police in a criminal investigation is a serious matter," said Henry. "And in law, newspaper reporters have no privileged position, though they have some sort of special consideration by long usage. But criminal investigation? Into what? When I saw you a couple of days ago, admittedly you told me you were keeping an open mind. But I took it that, following your investigations into the question of the keys, you had definitely ruled out the possibility of Miles Cabral having been murdered."

"I said a criminal investigation, not a murder investigation."

"Some other crime?" asked Henry, surprised.

Comfort slowly turned his gaze towards Kate. "You also wrote in this morning's newspaper that the police have re-opened their enquiries. I do not propose to ask how you came to know that."

Kate assured him, "My information did not come from any member of the police force. I give you my word."

She saw Henry suppressing a smile.

"You were not entirely right," Comfort told her. "You implied that the police have come round to your view that Mr. Cabral's death was not suicide. But that is not so. What I am enquiring into now is something different." He looked at her doubtfully. "Will you undertake to treat what I now tell you as off the record, not for publication?"

"From the police, yes, of course, I won't use anything you tell me now unless at some stage you give me permission to do so."

"I'm glad. Because I want some help from your husband." He turned to Henry. "When you looked at Mr. Cabral's coin collection that evening, you said there were three very optimistic spaces left—spaces for coins so rare that he could hardly hope ever to get them."

"Yes. A 1933 penny, a 1954 penny and an Edward VIII threepenny piece."

"A colleague of mine, a member of the Fraud Squad, told me yesterday that he has some indication that there is in operation a well-organized fraudulent sale, for very large sums of money, of counterfeit rare coins. One is said to be a 1954 penny.

"My colleague received information, through one of the channels he keeps open, that a collector in this country paid upwards of forty thousand pounds for this coin. He then detected a minute flaw on the reverse side and had it examined by experts. Best counterfeit they'd ever seen, apparently. The technicalities are beyond me, but I gather that the counterfeit must have been made by modern techniques of pressure-casting, whatever they may be, and that the density of the metal is almost exactly right. That'll mean more to you than it does to me, sir. What it amounts to is that it's a near-perfect counterfeit."

"Who's the collector?" asked Henry, full of curiosity.

"That we don't yet know. The information didn't come from him, but from a source known to the police. There could be several reasons why the man who was duped has not come forward."

"True," mused Henry. "He might have suspected it was stolen, or the money he paid for it might lead to awkward tax enquiries. He may have exported currency illegally to pay for it, or brought it surreptitiously through Customs."

"Or he might be proposing to sell it again to some other dupe, and regain his cash," said Comfort. "But that's not all. My colleague in the Fraud Squad had a private phone call from his opposite number in New York. An American collector had asked for an investigation into a sale to him, for more than ninety thousand dollars, of a very rare British coin which, on test, was found to be counterfeit."

"What coin?" asked Henry.

"A 1933 English penny, sir. Said to have come from London. The New York police know who the man is who was defrauded, but are keeping him anonymous for obvious reasons. They wanted to know whether there was anything of the kind being investigated here. London seems to be the centre. That's why my colleague came to me, knowing that I have been concerned with the enquiry into the death of Miles Cabral, a noted collector of rare coins.

"When I was told which coins had been counterfeited, I remembered what you had said about Mr. Cabral's three optimistic spaces. But there was absolutely nothing to connect Mr. Cabral's collection with the suspected fraud. But then Mrs. Theobald wrote in the *Post* this morning about people coming and going from Mr. Cabral's house on the afternoon of his death. I'm sure you understand that I must look into this. I have to have the identity of the young couple who, I feel sure, are the source of your information."

Kate said nothing.

Henry leaned forward.

"Mr. Comfort, it happens that I was with my wife when this information was given. I am not a newspaper reporter. So there is no reason why I should not tell you that the young man is an actor named Jonathan Parr, and the young woman, named Rosemary Ward, is living with him. At one time she was Miles Cabral's mistress.

"The reason they went to see Cabral, and what they were arguing about, was their belief that he had cheated Rosemary out of precisely those three coins, from a small collection left to her by her uncle. I don't know the uncle's name. Not Ward. But he had worked in the Mint, and left there in 1954.

"Because the street was dark, they cannot identify either the man who came out of the house with Cabral, or the man who later came down the street and entered one of the houses. They are not even certain that it was Cabral's house."

Kate said, "Henry advised Jonathan to come to you at the Yard this morning and volunteer what information he has. I would not give him to you as my source. But since Henry has, I will tell you what I have learned from the paper's own correspondents, provided you undertake not to pass on the information to any other reporters."

Comfort slowly smiled. "Undertook."

"First our man in the Channel Islands, whom I asked to look into Cabral's off-shore company in Guernsey. It had links with a small bank in Beirut. So I got in touch with our man in Lebanon. He found that Cabral seems to have owned the bank, which has been transferred to Damascus because of the fighting in Beirut. He also found that the bank's major depositor, whom Cabral always met on his frequent visits to Beirut, was a silversmith named Fouad Hakim."

Comfort raised his head suddenly. "Silversmith?"

"I thought Miles Cabral was using him as an agent to sell rare coins discreetly on the millionaire-collector market, world-wide. But if there's a question of counterfeits, then well, a silversmith . . . Now you've got to admit, Chief Inspector, that I'm not altogether an irresponsible citizen, even if I am a newspaper reporter."

"Freely admitted, Mrs. Theobald. Is there any more you can tell me?"

Kate saw Henry lean forward and knew he wanted to tell the policeman of Hakim's relatives in London, and what he suspected about her mugging. But she flickered a frown at him, and he remained silent.

"Nothing more, Chief Inspector," she said.

*   *   *

George Roseveare was punctual for his lunch date at
Henry's club. They could not discuss anything in the crowd
at the bar. When they were settled in the dining-room—
the coffee-room, as the club by tradition insisted on calling
it—Henry suggested George should give him a brief outline
of his position, to aid him when he came to the figures.

"I haven't brought them," replied George cheerfully.
"Most grateful for your offer of help, but this morning I
managed to fix everything up in another way. So I shan't
have to trouble you or your wife."

"Congratulations."

"I don't have to tell you what an enormous relief it is.
This is a delirious day for me, after months, years of the
most terrible anxiety. There were times when, if it hadn't
been for Angela, I think I might have done myself in."

"Was it that bad?"

"No risk of a criminal charge, if that's what you mean.
I managed to keep clear of that, though sometimes it was
a near thing. There are accountants who, for a consideration . . . oh well, never mind. It's over, finished, done
with."

"You got the substantial City backing you needed to
persuade Cabral's executors to fund your debts?"

"Substantial indeed. Couple of hundred thousand was
the lowest guarantee they'd consider, even though I had
that information about Cabral's affairs that Cornelius Ball
had given to Angela." He grinned cheerfully. "Blackmail,
old man. Thoroughly recommend it. Nothing like it for
getting you out of real trouble."

Henry asked, "Was it so much?"

George gently whistled. "What a rogue that man was.
If he were still alive, Cornelius could have got him gaoled
for years. I'm sure that's why he bumped himself off."

"Illegal export of currency?"

"In quite huge sums. Where the devil he got it all from,
when the property market collapsed, I can't imagine."

"Exported through that company in Guernsey?"

"That's right. Somewhere out to the Middle East. It
entailed, of course, a certain amount of corruption. That
alone, if proved, would have sent him down. And Cornelius almost certainly could have proved it. Great man,
that."

"Never met him," said Henry, "though Kate has."

"What would be of extra help," George considered,

"would be an item in a City newspaper column saying that I'm on my feet again. Would your wife mention that to her City office?"

"Depends," said Henry cautiously, "on your convincing me that you really are. They'd have to have something they could check, such as the name of your City backer."

"Forget it, old man. It isn't a City backer, as a matter of fact. Oh, why shouldn't I tell you—in confidence? I'm bursting with it. It's Cornelius Ball. He got back to London last night and came round to see us this morning. He'd been to the Middle East, where he has interests still.

"As it happens, Angela was feeling terribly low, what with the play closing, and my predicament. She spilled the whole thing out to Cornelius. He's very fond of her, not that way, not sexually, if you see what I mean. It's that she was so close to his sister, and has been looking after the child and all that. So he told her not to worry, and he and I went into another room and I told him exactly how I stand. He's putting up a personal guarantee of two hundred thousand. Isn't that marvellous?

"In fact, it won't cost him a sou. I swear to that. Property values are coming back. Why else do you think Cabral wanted to foreclose on mine, quite aside from spite about Angela? He knew damn well that in a year or two those properties would pay off. And they will. Once the mortgages have been funded into a long-term debt, I've no worries about the future. And of course Cornelius realizes that too. He's not so fond of Angela that he'd put up two hundred thousand for a bankrupt situation. An astute business man is Cornelius. And one of the finest men I've ever known."

CHAPTER 13

Kate was in the office that afternoon when Henry phoned.

"The lunch with George Roseveare?" she asked. "Is he in a complete bog?"

"No. He's out. He has found a backer, so he doesn't need Frank's help—unless he can shove in a paragraph in his City column hinting that George is solving his difficulties."

"Who's the backer?"

"He told me in confidence."

"Damn. Then it's no use asking Frank for even a paragraph. All I'll do is tip him off and let him find the story for himself. He'll soon do that, if it's true."

"It's true all right."

"Is it? In confidence then, who's the backer?"

"Cornelius Ball. He is backing George with a personal guarantee of two hundred thousand."

Kate was silent for a moment, then muttered that she ought to have guessed. She would ring Frank.

"Is Cornelius back in London?"

"Got back last night. He went round to see Angela this morning, found her in the dumps, heard about George, and offered the guarantee. According to George, he's not really risking anything. Once he has the financing of his properties on a reasonable basis, in a year or two they'll pick up their value and all will be well—says George."

"Do you believe that, Henry?"

"Could be. I really haven't enough information to say. See you this evening?"

"Probably, though I'm not quite sure how late I'll be. If I'm not in by eight, get yourself some supper, darling."

Cornelius back in London, she thought to herself when she had hung up the phone, and in generous mood. So he had evidently done satisfactorily whatever he went to

Beirut to do—or rather to Damascus, where he had phoned to Angela. Would he talk? He might, she told herself.

Americans start drinking at five-thirty; she remembered Cornelius had said so. She left it until nearly six, then took a taxi to the Connaught Hotel.

"I'm to meet Mr. Cornelius Ball here," she told the hall porter.

He replied, discreetly, that he would enquire whether Mr. Ball were in the hotel.

A few minutes later Cornelius came into the front hall from the bar, smiling. "You have a real knack for finding me, Mrs. Theobald. What can I do for you?"

"Tell me what you discovered in Beirut and Damascus."

"What I discovered? My dear lady, I was on a business trip. I did some business. Why should it interest you?"

"Because the business concerned Miles Cabral. You as good as told me so when I was leaving the cottage. You said you were confident of out-of-court settlements in New York and London, no matter where he had willed his money. That left the bank is Damascus. I took it that you went to plug that escape route too."

Cornelius murmured that she was acute. Possibly the business was something of that kind. It was not difficult in Syria to put through almost any business arrangement, provided you had the right contacts—and enough money.

"But what really interests me," went on Kate, "is the Beirut part of your business trip. You must have gone to see Fouad Hakim, and I think I know why."

Ball looked uneasy, not quite preventing himself glancing around as though to make sure that nobody was listening.

"I warned you not to pursue that," he said quietly. "Please believe that I meant that warning. Meant it most emphatically. Mrs. Theobald, do not, I beg you, get involved in anything to do with Hakim. There are considerations of which you know nothing . . ."

"That Fouad Hakim is a coin counterfeiter?' she asked.

He took hold of her arm, again looking uneasily round at other people in the vestibule. There were several groups, and people wandering in and out.

"What do you know about that?"

"Something."

"Better not talk about it here," he said. "My apartment is only a short walk away. I suggest we go there." He smiled. "I'll mix you my own special martini."

Kate hesitated. He noticed that and laughed.

"Don't be alarmed, Mrs. Theobald. Mrs. Horton and Cedric are at the apartment. You'll be adequately chaperoned."

The apartment was in Clarges Street, on the second floor. Ball switched on the hall light and showed Kate in. The sitting-room was in darkness; a small room, delightfully furnished, she saw, as he switched on the lights there too.

"I'll get some ice from the kitchen," he said, "and we'll have our martinis."

Kate looked around while he was out of the room. She felt uneasy; the flat in darkness, no sign of Mrs. Horton. But perhaps she was in whatever room was being used as the child's nursery.

Ball came back with a small ice-barrel and went to a corner cupboard to mix the drinks.

"Why have you brought Cedric to London?" she asked.

"I'm sending him and Mrs. Horton to the States. I've rented a small hideaway on Long Island." He came over with the drinks. "Newspaper reporters over there are not so sharp as you have them in London."

Kate sipped the martini; certainly dry, practically neat gin, slightly flavoured. "When are they going?"

Ball looked at her in dismay. "Good heavens, I've brought you here under false pretences. I've been in the City all day. I was thinking they were to fly tomorrow, but it's today. Forgive me."

"That's all right, Mr. Ball," she said, more staunchly than she felt. "Now, what about Hakim?"

"Let's sit down," he suggested, waving her to a chair on one side of the hearth, taking one himself on the other. "You said you know he is a counterfeiter. I won't ask how you know. But you're right. I'll tell you how I found out, and you must publish if you think fit. I've no objection, but your newspaper lawyers may have. And my advice to you is, don't. As I've warned you, that could be very dangerous."

"It'll be up to me and my editor. So how did you find out?"

"You remember we spoke of a 1954 penny at our luncheon meeting at the Connaught. You had hinted in your newspaper that Cabral might have one, but you told me it was not in his coin cabinet. So I wondered if there were any news of it among the dealers. I'm well known in those circles, so I postponed my departure to New York for twenty-four hours, and next day I was directed, with great caution, to a dealer from whom I had bought once before. To my delight, he produced the 1954 penny, and I bought it for rather more than forty thousand pounds."

"Was the dealer Mr. Foskett?"

"No, no. I know Harvey Foskett well, of course, and have often bought from him. In fact, I bought the Charles I crown for which Cabral outbid me—and for less than it fetched at that auction. So Harvey got most of his money back. No, this other dealer hasn't Harvey's high reputation. But he did have the 1954 penny. I took it back to New York, and showed it proudly to my experts. It was counterfeit. Wonderfully done, but not quite perfect.

"My experts said it almost certainly came from Beirut, which is the centre for this sort of thing. My business agent in Tripoli made a few enquiries and reported that the most likely source was a silversmith named Fouad Hakim in Beirut—and he warned me about certain dangers. Which was why I warned you."

Kate wondered whether to tell him about the mother and her grandson in London, and the time she got mugged. But decided not to—not yet, anyway.

"I was going to Damascus," Ball went on, "to get Cabral's bank assets frozen, as you rightly surmised. So I also went to see this silversmith. He admitted the counterfeit penny was his work. Why not? It's not illegal in Lebanon. So I asked where he got the original. You have to have an original coin, of course, to be able to make a counterfeit. He said that, as Cabral was dead, he didn't mind telling me. He got it from Cabral. 'As usual,' he said."

"You mean," asked Kate, "that Cabral . . .?"

"Exactly. Cabral had been running for years a fraud with counterfeits of rare coins. It must have been how he first got capital to launch into business."

"From counterfeit coins? But surely they wouldn't have produced that kind of money."

"Oh, but they would," Ball assured her. "I managed to get a few of the details from Hakim, though he closed up when I tried to find how the coins were marketed. Not by him, I'm fairly sure, but through a dealer or dealers in London. It's probably a network."

"Including the man who sold you the 1954 penny?"

"Possibly."

"Then why not go to the police?"

"I think I may," he said, "when I have found out enough to be sure. But you asked about the profits. Cabral concentrated on coins which could be sold only to top-level collectors, mostly American, German or Swiss, for around thirty thousand dollars each—say fifteen thousand pounds. He must have started with less costly coins, but that was the level he had worked up to. When he bought one such coin, at auction, say, he took it or sent it to Hakim, who made usually ten counterfeit copies. These were sent back to Cabral with the dies, which he destroyed, and the original coin, so he got his outlay back.

"The ten copies were then marketed slowly, unobtrusively, in several parts of the world, to bring in about one hundred and fifty thousand. He paid Hakim a fixed sum for each operation, and the marketing agents were probably on a percentage. But it's unlikely that Cabral himself pocketed less than a hundred thousand for no outlay, tax free, and much of it outside the currency restrictions of the sterling area. Ten operations would have made him a secret, tax-free million pounds, Mrs. Theobald. And he had been at it for years."

Kate drew in her breath. "I wonder how much of that I dare print."

"Print it all, so far as I am concerned."

"May I quote you?"

"No, I fear not."

"Then what authority have I? Only your word."

He smiled. "Not good enough for you?"

"Should it be? The first time we met you told me something that wasn't true."

He frowned. "I did not lie to you."

"To me," she insisted, "and to the police. You said that when you went to Miles Cabral's house that afternoon you could get no answer at the door. Was that true, Mr. Ball?"

He was silent for a moment. Then he spoke as smoothly and calmly as ever.

"I read your report in the *Post* this morning. Two men entered the house. You think I was one of them?"

"Don't forget that I interviewed the young couple who saw one man leave and the other arrive."

Another silence. Then Ball sighed. "All right. I did see Cabral. It was about Cedric. I told Cabral that he had to settle a million pounds on the child. It would no longer help him to sneer, as he had before, that he doubted the paternity. I now had enough about his illegal currency operations to get him a long gaol sentence. He said that Angela had threatened him with the same thing that afternoon. What evidence had I got? I told him and it obviously shook him. I gave him one month to set up a trust for Cedric, or I'd go to the authorities. Then I left."

"What time did you leave?"

Ball sighed again. "You have detected a second lie. I told you, and the police, that I went to the house at five-thirty. I saw the young couple in the street when I left. There was a chance they might report having seen a man leave, so I made out that I had arrived half an hour later than I actually had. I got to the house at five, and left after about twenty minutes. I wasn't to know that another man would call at five-thirty and also be seen by that couple. That was sheer bad luck."

"Why did you lie, Mr. Ball?"

"I had most important business awaiting me in New York. If I admitted having actually talked to Cabral in his house, I should have had to stay in London for the inquest. So I lied. But it really wasn't of much consequence; the evidence I could have given would have made not the slightest difference to the verdict. He was seen to be alive after I left him. Missing those New York conferences could have cost me heavily. The lies did no harm to anyone, and saved me from a possible large business loss. Now, will you print that?"

Kate said, "How can I? You would deny it, and again it would be my word against yours. And of course, as you say, your call at the house doesn't throw any fresh light on Cabral's death."

"Splendid," he said. But she could see from the sudden shrewd look in his eyes that he doubted her. "Then let's forget it," he said. "I'm going to mix another drink." He went to the corner cupboard. "Damn. I left the lid off the ice-barrel and the ice has melted. But I have more. Will you join me in another?"

"Love to," said Kate.

That, she told herself, was her tactical lie. Suppose he had been the second man at Cabral's house, not the first. Suppose, about that, he had now lied to her again, because . . . well, because if anybody killed Cabral it must have been the second caller.

She had the wild thought that he could slip a knockout drop into her next drink. Was that what he was leaving the room to get, not more ice?

And after, when she was unconscious . . . For she was the only person who knew he had been in that house. If silence were vital to him, she was the person to be silenced.

So she told her lie.

"Love to," she said.

"But don't make it such a strong one as the last," she called after him as he went to the kitchen for more ice. She forced herself to giggle. "Are you trying to get me soused, Mr. Ball?"

As she said it, she crossed the room as fast as she could without making a noise, crept into the hall, opened the flat door and fled in panic down the stairs into the street.

A taxi was passing. She gave her home address and sat back on the seat, taut. Not until the taxi had mingled with the Piccadilly traffic did she relax. She found she was gasping.

Luckily Henry was already home.

He saw she looked upset. "Anything the matter?"

"I don't know. I may have just been silly, and panicked. But I was damn frightened."

"Tell me."

She told him briefly. "Now, what do you think? Was I getting into a state and imagining things? Because if not, it must be Cornelius Ball who killed Miles Cabral."

"Sit down quietly," said Henry, "and let's see. He admits he was lying when he said he got to Cabral's house at five-thirty and could get no response. In fact he got there at five and Cabral let him in. He came out twenty minutes later. But that exonerates him, surely. Jonathan and Rosemary saw Cabral come out with him, and they themselves spoke to Cabral after he had gone."

"Unless he was lying again, Henry. Unless he was the man who got there at five-thirty, the second man the youngsters saw, and Cabral admitted him then. We've only his word for the timing."

"Are you suggesting, not only that he shot Cabral, but that he stole those three coins?"

"No. That wouldn't fit. If he had taken those coins, why would he have asked me to meet him at lunch to find out if Cabral really had a 1954 penny? His quarrel with Cabral wasn't about coins. It was about his sister and the child."

"The gun," mused Henry. "How did he know about Cabral's revolver being in the drawer of the desk in the coins room?"

"It must have been Cabral who produced the gun. Cornelius was threatening him with criminal charges, with gaol. Cabral knew Fred Sharp could probably steal the evidence from Angela's flat. But Cornelius had much more. Would you have put it past Cabral to have realized that the only way out was to kill him?" A sudden thought came to her. "Didn't Rosemary say the second caller was carrying a briefcase? Perhaps Cornelius brought some of the most damning evidence with him, to confront Cabral with."

"Seems unlikely. Why take such a risk? Photocopies would do."

"Do stop making difficulties, darling," Kate protested. "Somehow Cornelius got hold of the gun and shot Cabral. He had plenty of time to get away. We didn't reach the house until eight minutes past six."

"And the burglar alarm?"

"Damn the burglar alarm," she replied irritably. "There's got to be an answer to that."

"This counterfeiting thing," said Henry. "It's credible, you know. Modern techniques have made it possible to produce almost perfect copies of specific coins, and Beirut seems to be the place. When I went to see Harvey Foskett, he warned me that the coin I was pretending to offer him had been frequently counterfeited. He reminded me that the coins that landed an American in a Swiss gaol a few years ago were counterfeits made in Lebanon. I'd read of it at the time, the coin magazines were full of it. If I run into Harvey, I'll ask him if there's another spate of copies. He knows everything that's going on in the trade." Henry laughed. "If it's true, there must be dozens of prized coins in the cabinets of the wealthiest collectors that are fakes, worthless. Is that really possible?"

"There are dozens of fake Old Masters and modern oils hanging in public galleries all over the world," Kate pointed out, "according to that chap in Minorca, forget his name, who claimed he had painted them and sold them to the foremost experts."

"There's a difference. You can paint a picture in the manner of an Old Master or a modern. It doesn't have to be an exact copy of a known painting. In fact, it mustn't be. To forge a rare coin you have to start with the original." Henry suddenly stared. 'So, if Cornelius Ball has a fake 1954 penny, what about an original?"

"In Rosemary's uncle's little collection," answered Kate. "Miles Cabral got it, Fred Sharp must have taken it to Hakim in Beirut, and Hakim probably still has it."

"Then how did the fake get back to London for Ball to buy?"

"Maybe Hakim's son delivered it."

"To whom?"

"To the dealer Cabral had been using."

Henry dissented. "Won't wash, Kate. One thing is certain. If Cabral was running a long-term fraud on that scale, he would never have allowed his coiner to have the slightest knowledge of marketing arrangements."

"There's no point in trying to guess about that, Henry. What we have to decide is what we do about Cornelius. I feel pretty sure he killed Cabral. But how can I go to the police? All I could say is that I got frightened, I thought he was going to kill me, so I ran."

"What you can and indeed must tell Comfort is that Ball has a counterfeit 1954 penny. The police know a collector paid more than forty thousand for it, but they don't know his identity. You can't keep that to yourself. It could be the key to uncovering the whole thing. The network must still be in operation, for Ball to have been taken for a sucker."

"All right," Kate agreed reluctantly. For she knew very well there was nothing here she could print. But she could probably reckon on Comfort giving her a few hours' beat when anything could go to the Press.

"I'll ring Mr. Comfort tomorrow," she promised.

"You'll ring him tonight, my girl, or I will."

The phone rang. Henry took it.

"Yes, she's here." He handed over the phone. "It's Butch, for you."

"I'm speaking from home, Kate. I've just had a call from

the night news desk. There's been another Arab shooting in Mayfair. Can you get to the office straight away?"

"Why, Butch? What's it got to do with me?"

"It's an American—that millionaire, Cornelius Ball. You knew him, didn't you? He was gunned down as he came out of a building in Clarges Street where he has a flat. A couple of passers-by saw it happen. The gunman was standing in a doorway on the other side of the street. As Ball came out, he opened fire with a small automatic, probably Russian. Then he ran off into Piccadilly. The couple who saw him say he is a swarthy young man, looked like an Arab. I think it must be one of the extreme Palestinian groups. Ball used to be an ambassador somewhere out there, and he got politically and personally involved with a few of the moderate Arab leaders. The story is that he had just come back from a quick trip to Syria. There's already the idea that he was on an undercover mission for the U.S. Government. But there's nothing official. What we want is a personal piece by you as somebody who knew him."

"Is he badly hurt?" asked Kate faintly.

"Badly hurt? He's dead."

CHAPTER 14

The office was humming with energy. The first edition was just being tucked away. Kate saw that Butch himself had come in. He called her quickly.

"This is blowing up into one hell of a story, Kate. It's being said now that Ball had fixed up new peace talks between the Palestinians and the Lebanese. One commentator reckons he could have got close to an undercover Palestinian-Israel conference."

"Better send me home, Butch. I'll spoil your story."

"How? You know something?"

"I was with Cornelius Ball this evening, in his flat."

Butch stared at her. "Cripes! What were you doing there?"

"Following up the Miles Cabral story. I don't believe that Cornelius's killing had anything to do with politics. It's about rare coins."

Butch raised his eyebrows. "Come off it, Kate."

"The Yard has started an investigation into a big-scale international fraud, centred on London, in which millions are being made from counterfeit rare coins. The forgeries are done in Lebanon. The police know that a wealthy collector recently paid forty thousand for a 1954 penny to a London dealer. They don't know yet who the dealer is, and nor do I. They also don't know the identity of the collector. Or perhaps they do now. Henry has gone to the Yard to tell them. It was Cornelius Ball. The man who was operating the fraud until his death was Miles Cabral. It's how he made his original millions, and probably how he survived the property slump."

"Can you write all that?"

"Why not? Now he's dead, Cornelius can't contradict me," she said throatily.

Butch touched her arm. "Are you feeling all right? Were you involved with him?"

She shook her head. "It's just damn difficult to take, that a man you were having a drink with in his flat this very evening was murdered on his doorstep not long after. I could have been coming out of that doorway with him. But I'm all right, Butch. Bit shaken, that's all. I can write it. Tough girl reporter, that's me."

"Want me to take you over to the Scriveners for a stiffener before you start?"

"No. I'd better get on with it. I'll put in a black, and I want the copy filed straight away as a service message to Geoff Wilton in Beirut. Add one instruction. Upfollow Hakim fastest."

She went to her desk, pulled the typewriter before her and started, calling a boy to take each slip across to Butch as she finished it. Now and then she glanced across and saw Butch talking fast to the copy taster, handing him her typescript.

She felt a kind of numbness as she wrote, almost as though she had been stunned. So she had been, in a sense, she told herself. But she was damned if that would interfere with her story.

She took the last slip over herself.

"Are you still going to run the political angle?" she asked Butch.

"We'll tuck a short piece by the diplomatic correspondent somewhere, just to cover in case something confirmatory turns up. But it's your piece we're going on, Kate. Nobody's going to have anything to touch that tomorrow. It'll go round the world. The Yanks are clamouring madly. After all, he was their millionaire, ex-ambassador and, according to the wildest of the think-pieces coming through on the tapes, their presidential undercover man for Middle East peace."

She shrugged apathetically. All she wanted was to get home and crawl into bed.

"As for you," Butch went on, "you're taking a week's holiday."

"Not much."

"Yes you are. You look done in. I've already talked to Henry about it. When? Just now. He phoned. He agrees. He'll take you off tomorrow to a little pub he knows in Devon. Inglenooks with big log fires, a snug bar, the publican's wife doing the cooking—one of the best cooks in England, Henry reckons."

"I know the place," Kate told him. "I'm not going."

"Well, you must argue that out with Henry. But a week's holiday you will certainly take. That's an order."

"Oh, shut up, Butch. I'm not in the mood for the jovial manner. I'm going home."

"Sit down, girl. Henry told me you hadn't eaten, so I've had these sent over from the Scriveners."

He pushed a plate of ham sandwiches to her across the desk.

"I'll eat when I get home."

"And a large Scotch," he added, lifting the glass over. "Henry's coming to pick you up. He said he'd come in the car, so he shouldn't be long."

"Tell him I've taken a taxi."

Butch looked serious. "Henry said that on no account was I to let you go off by yourself. He said to tie you up if you proved difficult. So sit down, Kate, and have your sandwiches."

She slowly let herself down on to the chair. The sandwiches she could not touch, but the whisky was comforting.

"Why on earth should Henry have said that?"

"Something the police told him, maybe. He was phoning from the Yard."

The warning about danger to Kate had come at the end of Henry's session at the Yard.

When he first got there, he was just in time to catch Chief Inspector Comfort before he left for home.

"It's about Cornelius Ball. My wife was with him earlier this evening, at his flat, not long before the shooting. She knew nothing about that. She had gone before it happened. But she did learn a lot from Mr. Ball. And there are other things I must tell you."

Comfort sat down again at his desk, waving Henry into the chair opposite. He buzzed for Sergeant Chin.

"Ask Inspector Grierson if he will step over. Tell him it's relevant and important."

To Henry he said, "Detective Inspector Grierson has been seconded to a little outfit specializing in terrorism. I'd like him to sit in on whatever you have to say."

"I don't think it'll be what he expects," Henry said. "But by all means let's wait."

Inspector Grierson was a tall, thin man with large ears and sad brown eyes; a vaguely dog-like face. He looked at

Comfort for permission, then got out and filled an old, worn pipe.

"Now then, Mr. Theobald."

So Henry told them what Kate had learned from Cornelius Ball about the counterfeit fraud, about Hakim the silversmith, about Ball's allegation that the fraud had been run by Miles Cabral, who had made millions by it. He told them of Ball's admission that he had actually entered Cabral's house on the afternoon the man died, and of their altercation.

"He was the man whom Jonathan Parr and Rosemary Ward had seen coming out of the house with Cabral himself at about five-twenty—or so he said."

Then Henry told them that Kate had been mugged in that dim alley close to her newspaper office; of old Mrs. Hakim's phone calls to her, and visit to him; of the "wild" grandson.

"I thought at first she was just one of the nuts that newspapers attract," said Henry. "But when I got the significance of the name Hakim . . ."

Comfort asked Grierson, "Name mean anything to you?"

"Not a known terrorist, nor a known Palestinian of any sort."

Henry remembered. "The old woman told me it was one of the Lebanese Christian families."

"Then you can almost rule terrorism out," said Grierson.

"Any idea how long they've been in London?" Comfort asked Henry.

"None. But if young Hakim was acting as courier with that fake penny, presumably he came after Cabral's death."

"If they came as tourists," Comfort murmured, almost to himself, "they'd have filled in entry forms, passport numbers and all that, on the aircraft before landing." He turned to Chin. "Ask our contact with the Home Office computer. An elderly woman and a young man, they'll have filled in dates of birth, probably from Lebanon, both named Hakim. Go back a couple of months. See if there's a record."

While he was away they talked for a while, desultorily. Then Grierson stood up. "I'd better get back, sir. It's still much more likely to have been political, and nothing to do with any family of silversmiths. But if you do get anything firm . . ."

"Of course," said Comfort.

He and Henry continued to wait.

"By the way, where is Mrs. Theobald now, sir? Oh, silly of me. I don't have to ask. She is in her newspaper office, writing tomorrow's front page."

"A good deal of it, I expect. There's no way of stopping her, Mr. Comfort."

Comfort smiled thinly. "By now I know that."

At last Chin returned, holding a sheet of paper.

"They came in at Heathrow on a Middle East Airways flight on the twenty-fourth of last month, sir. Mrs. Rachel Hakim, aged seventy-two, and Nasib Hakim, aged twenty. The London address they gave was a small hotel in Kensington. I phoned the hotel, sir. They checked out on the twenty-eighth, no forwarding address."

"Have you tried the Kensington police?"

"Put through a request, sir. They don't think they have anything."

Comfort turned to Henry. "In the light of what you have told me, I think your wife is in considerable danger, especially if it appears in tomorrow morning's *Post* that she was with Cornelius Ball shortly before he was killed. Get her to hold out any such report. She can print it later."

"I'll try," murmured Henry doubtfully. He knew very well that he would not succeed.

"She may have stumbled on a major criminal organization. Whether Cabral had anything to do with it is simply not proven at this stage, though it seems possible. What is certain is that the organization still exists and is ready to use murder as a protective weapon. Your wife was knocked down in the street as a warning not to go on probing. I think you are probably right, her assailant was Nasib Hakim. It's possible that the same man shot Mr. Ball this evening. I don't have to elaborate the danger to Mrs. Theobald, do I?"

Henry asked to use his phone and got through to the news desk at the *Post*. "That you, Butch? I'm speaking from the Yard. Will you please hold out Kate's report from tomorrow's paper? She'll be in grave danger if it's printed."

"Sorry, old boy. Too late. We fudged it briefly in the first edition as it was running. Then we replated page one, and that's now running on the machines. Even if I wanted to, I couldn't recall several thousand copies from the distributors. And of course our hated rivals will have pounced on the first copies to hit the street. The Yanks will have filed it to New York by now."

"Then don't let Kate leave the office alone. I'll pick up my car and come and fetch her. Tie her up if you have to, Butch. I'm really not joking."

"Is it that serious?"

"The police think it could be. Insist that she goes on holiday tomorrow. I'll take her to a splendid little pub in Devon. Very cosy in the winter, log fires and all that, and the wife cooks wonderfully."

"Get that address from you some time, old boy," said Butch.

Kate absolutely refused. She wouldn't argue about it to-night, she said, when Henry got her back to the flat, she was tired out. In the morning she was just as adamant. Nothing would make her hide herself away in Devon, or anywhere else, while all this was going on.

"Don't be so intrepid, Kate. It doesn't suit you."

"Intrepid? I'm scared breathless. Don't worry, I'm not taking any risks. I've phoned Butch, and he's sending round an office car, with Sam driving. I'll go in that. And Sam'll look after me. He's no slouch. Anybody around with a machine-gun, Sam'll do him."

"It isn't funny, Kate."

"Of course it isn't, darling. I'll take care."

A car hooted in the street below. She looked out of the window.

"There's Sam now. I'm only going to the office. See you tonight."

Making for the door, Henry said he was going down first, to make sure everything was all right.

"This is London," she protested.

"Clarges Street is in London," he reminded her grimly.

It was an office car, and Sam greeted him. Henry told him quickly that there was danger for Kate, but she insisted on going out.

"I know. The news desk warned me. I'll look after her, Mr. Theobald."

When they had gone, Henry walked slowly back up-stairs, pondering. The only sure way to remove the danger was to remove the assailant. If the police could grab young Hakim, they'd probably have the lot of them in the bag, and that would be that.

He sat down and telephoned the Yard, asking for Chief Inspector Comfort.

"Sergeant Chin here, sir. Mr. Comfort's not in the office."

"Have you found Hakim yet?"

"Not yet, sir. This town's swarming with Arabs. But never fear, we'll get him soon."

"Let me know the moment you do, please."

There seemed no way in which he could help, so he took the Underground from Sloane Square to the Temple and went to his chambers. He was not in court that day, but had a brief to read all morning.

It was a cold day, but dry, so he put on his heavy overcoat and a scarf round his neck and walked to his club for lunch. On the way, he turned his mind back to the Hakim problem. He tried to remember every detail of the old woman's visit to him in the flat, her arrival in rain-sodden coat and shawl, her urgency and anguish. Her look of terror when he suggested talking to her grandson, groping her way out, in the still wet coat and shawl he fetched her from the kitchen. She would not let him get her a taxi, even though he tried to offer her the fare. What was it exactly she had said? She would go by bus. No. 31. He had protested that she would have to go to the other end of King's Road to catch that service, but she had swathed herself in that sopping shawl and gone slowly, arthritically, down the stairs.

The bus. No. 31. Was that a pointer? If that was the bus to take her home, then she was living somewhere along its route—the west end of Chelsea, through Earls Court, then Kensington proper, and nearly to Hampstead. He whistled to himself in despair; a route across the heart of a large city. Not much of a pointer after all.

Then he remembered Jim Greenhurst, old college friend, now in the foreign service, who usually lunched at the club.

He asked the porter if Mr. Greenhurst was in. Yes, sir, in the bar. Henry hung up his coat and went to find him.

"Hallo, Henry, what'll you drink?"

"Thanks. Just a small can. Jim, I wonder if you can help me. I'm trying to locate a Lebanese family, probably somewhere along the route served by the thirty-one bus."

Greenhurst pulled a face. "Chelsea, Earls Court, North Kensington, through to Hampstead. There are more Arabs living along that route, old son, than off the Kasr el Nil.

I suppose it's something to do with Kate's report in the *Post* this morning. Yes, of course I read it. Fascinating stuff. A Lebanese family living along the thirty-one bus route, eh? Tell you what, there's a fellow works along the corridor from me who specializes in the Lebanese. I'll have a word with him when I get back there this afternoon. Where will you be? In chambers?"

"Yes. Call me if your fellow has any pointers, will you?"

"Sure. Here's your beer."

It was mid-afternoon before Greenhurst phoned.

"Henry, is the family Muslim or Christian?"

"Christian."

"Hold on a minute. I'm in my colleague's office and that's what he wanted to know."

Henry waited, hearing a dim conversation at the other end of the line. Then Jim again; "My chap says there used to be a little Maronite group in Earls Court, some of them Syrian, but some from Lebanon. Did a spot of propaganda. But he hasn't heard anything from them for a while. He thinks the money ran out, and he doesn't know if they're still there. They used to have a small office in Warwick Road, fairly close to the Underground entrance. He can't remember the house number, but it was in a basement. Hope that's of some use."

A slim chance, thought Henry, as he got into his heavy overcoat and wound his scarf round his neck. It was cold outside, overcast, gloomy. But the slimmest chance was better than none.

He took a district train to Earls Court and emerged into Warwick Road; terrace houses, all cut up now into flats or bedsitters. There was no indication on any of the nearby basement doors, so he descended the steps into one area to enquire. A blonde came to the door. She evidently wore a dressing-gown at tea-time. He asked her if she knew of a small Lebanese group with an office in one of the basements. Lots of bloody Arabs two doors along, she told him, jerking her thumb to the left.

A short, swarthy man opened that basement door.

"I'm looking for a Mrs. Hakim," said Henry. "She came to see me, to ask me to do something for her grandson. I've done what she asked and I can't remember the address she gave me."

The man regarded him in silence. Henry thought he was going to shut the door on him. But then he told him to wait there. The man retreated into the front room of the basement. Through the grimy window, Henry could just make out that he was telephoning.

After a few minutes he saw him leave the phone off the hook. Then he reappeared at the door. "Your name. What is it?"

"Mr. Theobald."

The man returned to the telephone. After a while he emerged again, locked the door behind him and pointed up the steps.

"Mrs. Hakim. I take you."

He led the way the short distance to Nevern Square, and into a house on the far side. Henry followed him up two flights of stairs. He knocked on a flat door. It was opened by another swarthy man, who muttered something to the first in their own language. Then the second man opened the door wider and motioned to Henry to enter.

As he stepped into the dim hall of the flat, the first man suddenly shoved him hard in the back. Henry stumbled, just saved himself from falling.

As he turned, the door closed. The first man suddenly gripped his arm and twisted it behind. Henry was about to throw him off and fight his way out, when the second man drew a knife and held it against his throat.

"Go in."

There was no alternative. He stumbled down the hall, his shoulders bowed forward by the arm twisted behind him. Through an open door of a room on the left he caught a glimpse of the old woman, Mrs. Hakim. He thought she was weeping.

CHAPTER 15

Kate was bored at the office. Nothing seemed to be happening and there was nothing she could do. Her story was gratifyingly spread over most of page one of that morning's paper. But what was to follow? There was no particular lead. The police had clammed up, so had the Foreign Office. Think-pieces were streaming in on the agency tapes, from Washington, from Damascus, from Cairo, but they were all speculation, guesses.

The Americans were starting to discard her counterfeit coins motive and to revert to politics. How could it be anything but? An American ex-ambassador, once deeply involved in the Middle East situation, just back from a secret journey to Lebanon and Syria, gunned down in a London street by a Palestinian terrorist. Open and shut. The fanciful idea of a criminal organization had been a good lead from London, but the Americans simply disbelieved it. They were accustomed, after all, to fanciful Mafia stories. This was politics, particularly as the White House had refused to comment.

"Oh hell," said Kate to Butch. "Can't you find me anything to do?"

"You should be on holiday, Kate. I told you." He looked at his watch. "Come over to the Scriveners. I'll be your bodyguard, and we can take Sam too."

The lift was busy, so they walked down the stairs. Near the bottom of the second flight somebody had dropped a corded bundle of that morning's edition. The staircase was dimly lit, Kate was talking to Butch. She caught her foot on the bundle and went tumbling on to the landing.

Butch quickly picked her up. "You all right, girl? This damned staircase. We've complained often enough about the lighting, and the bloody management does nothing."

He set her down on her feet, and she yelped.

"Twisted my ankle. Damn."

She tried to walk but could manage only a hobble.

"Do you think you've broken it?" asked Butch in dismay. "Hang on to that rail while I get the lift. And this settles it, girl. I'm putting you in the car, Sam will take you to your doctor, and then home. And don't you dare come near the office. When Henry gets back, humble yourself and tell him to take you to that pub in Devon."

"Damn, damn, damn."

As he put her in the car, Butch said, "When you get home, lock the door and don't answer to anyone. I'm serious, Kate. Just for once, do as you're told."

"I want to know what's happening."

"I'll phone you from time to time."

Her doctor was reassuring. "It's all right, Mrs. Theobald. Your ankle isn't broken. Only a bad sprain. I'll bind it, and try not to walk on it more than you can help for a few days. If it's no better in a couple of days, come to see me again. But I don't think it'll give you much trouble. Bit painful now, of course."

Sam was in the waiting-room. He helped her out to the car and drove her home. "How are you going to manage all those stairs?"

"I can hobble up by grasping the handrail."

"Better not," said Sam.

He lifted her bodily and carried her up.

"Oh, Sam! You'll have a heart attack. At my weight!"

"Sunday cyclist. Do a club run of at least fifty miles every Sunday. Develops the leg muscles wonderful. My old woman says . . . But I'd better not tell you what my old woman says."

Once in the flat, she did lock and bolt the front door, feeling silly as she did so; but then reminding herself of Clarges Street. What would have happened, she asked herself for the umpteenth time, if she had stayed? Would Cornelius really have slipped something in her drink to knock her out, and then . . . And then what?

Had she panicked without reason? Then why the flat instead of talking in the hotel? Why the lie about Mrs. Horton and the child?

Moreover, she now felt quite sure that it was Cornelius who had killed Miles Cabral. He was the man who had arrived at five-thirty, the second man Jonathan and Rosemary had seen, not the first.

From the hall she took Henry's silver-knobbed walking stick. Leaning on this, now that her ankle was tightly bound, she could get around with fair comfort.

The phone rang. It was Butch. Yes, she was quite safe, she assured him, door locked and bolted. Her ankle was not broken, only sprained. Any developments about Cornelius Ball? None.

"I'll call you after lunch," Butch promised.

With nothing else to do, Kate started to go carefully over everything that had happened since that awful moment when she had opened the coins-room door and seen Miles Cabral's body lying on the floor, the gun on the carpet, the blood, the little heap of brain substance. Even now she shuddered slightly.

Going over the whole sequence reinforced her conviction that Cornelius Ball had killed him. Only one basic question remained. How did Cornelius get out of the house and set the perimeter burglar-alarm behind him?

He had to have two keys—to the control panel in the hall cupboard, and to the shunt lock in the front door. She boiled an egg for her lunch, read a book, dozed in front of the fire. Butch called a couple of times. She assured him she was all right. Every now and then she returned to the problem of the two keys Cornelius Ball must have had.

There were keys available to him, of course—Miles's own keys in his trousers pocket. He could reset the alarm with those from outside the house. But how did he then get the keys back into Miles's pocket?

Suddenly she saw a possibility that nobody had thought of.

She put on her thickest coat, for it was now late afternoon, the day was darkening and cold. With the help of Henry's walking stick she got down the stairs and on to the street. She knew of a small locksmith's shop in Fulham. She grabbed a taxi and, once at the shop, told the driver to wait for her.

"Keys Cut While You Wait," was the notice in the shop window.

She handed her own latch key to the locksmith and asked him to cut a copy. She watched as he fastened her key to one end of the small machine, and a blank key at the other end.

"How does it work?"

"Easy enough, miss. This here guide, which follows the outline of the pattern key, is linked to this here cutting wheel, which grinds out the same pattern on the blank. Don't take long."

"Mind if I time it?"

"Help yourself," he said, switching on the motor.

The cutting operation took just over two minutes. Adding the time for fixing the pattern key and the blank, the whole thing could scarcely have taken less than five minutes, probably more.

"Will it copy any key?" she asked the locksmith.

"Sure," he said, touching up the new key with a file where the cut was rough. "So long as it's not too big, and you've got the right blank."

"How big?"

"Usual size keys for doors," he answered, handing her the two keys and taking her money.

Back in the flat, after hauling herself up the stairs by the handrail, Kate reached for the Yellow Pages phone directory. The nearest locksmith to Cabral's house seemed to be quite a way off, in Pimlico. Even by car, it must take at least five minutes to get there, probably ten, and the return journey the same.

Cornelius had the use of Miles's keys for a very limited time. He arrived at the house at five-thirty. He knew that people were coming to drinks, could be at six. He could not possibly have shot Miles, taken his keys to the locksmith, had two cut and returned in time.

But there was an alternative. She would not tell anyone about that until late in the evening, when she would tell Henry and send him off to the police; and meanwhile phone her piece to the *Post*.

She began to rough it out. Cornelius went there with the intention of killing Miles. A well-planned murder.

Rosemary had noticed that he had been carrying something, a briefcase, she thought. One of the things it contained must have been his own revolver. He held Miles up with that, forced him into the coins room, put on rubber gloves, swiftly opened the desk drawers until he found Miles's own gun, shot him with that.

Also in the case he was carrying a key-cutting machine. Why not? There are portable typewriters, portable sewing-machines. A portable key-cutter would be smaller than that, and would need only to be plugged into an electric socket. Cornelius must have had a portable machine specially made, small and light; probably had it made in the States. He could have taken, say, twenty different-sized doorkey blanks for the shunt lock in the front door, and as many blanks about the size of car-door keys from which to cut a key for the alarm control-panel.

No doubt he had practiced with the machine, so that he had time to cut duplicates from Miles's own keys, which he then replaced in the trousers pocket.

So that was how it was done.

CHAPTER 16

At the end of the hallway down which Henry had been forced to walk, bent almost double with an arm twisted behind his back by the one man, and with a knife held at the side of his throat by the other, was a small kitchen. He was halted in its doorway.

"The other arm," grunted the man behind him.

At first Henry did not move, but the knife was scratched against his neck, making a slight cut. He put his other arm behind his back. He could feel a cord being tautened round his wrists, then knotted.

A moment later his legs were tripped so that he fell backwards to the floor. As one foot was grasped he began to kick with the other. But the man with the knife crouched by his side, menacing. So he lay still while the first man bound his ankles together.

Looking up, he could now see both men. The one with the knife was taller and younger than the man who had brought him to the flat. Both were swarthy. The knife-wielder, Henry judged, was the wild grandson, Nasib Hakim.

The door to a cupboard, just outside the kitchen door, was pulled open. Both men thrust him inside. With his back against the far wall and his legs drawn close in, knees bent, he occupied nearly all the floor space.

The younger man told him, "You stay there. If you make a noise, you are killed."

He shut the door. Henry heard a bolt closing on the outside, and the footsteps of the two men returning along the uncarpeted hallway.

Not long after, there was the sound of a door slamming. He thought it must be the front door of the flat. One of the men might have gone. One, he was sure, remained.

The cupboard was not in darkness. There was a dim

light through a small window high up in the back wall; evidently an outside wall. It showed a shelf, also high up, on which things were stacked. He could not quite make out what things. Leaning against a side wall of the cupboard were two brooms.

By pressing his feet against one side wall, and twisting his back round against the other, Henry managed to work himself upright. Feeling with his hands behind his back, he got hold of the handle of one of the brooms and gradually lifted it until it touched the bottom of the shelf. Then he thrust it sharply upwards. One side of the shelf split and several wine glasses fell on to his head, his shoulders, and then smashed on the floor.

After the noise of that he stood in silence, listening. There was a soft shuffle of feet in the hallway. Then, in almost a whisper, the old woman's voice. "Mr. Theobald. Please to be quiet, I beg you."

He answered in a low voice, "Your grandson did not hear that?"

"He has gone to the mister," she said. Her voice was tremulous. "To tell him you are here."

Henry was lowering himself again in the cupboard, until he could get hold of a piece of broken glass in one of his hands

"Who is this mister?"

There was no answer.

After a short while, as he tried to jam the pieces of glass into a crack between the wall and the skirting, Henry asked, "The other man is still here?"

"He is in the front room. I give him a meal."

The glass seemed to be holding sufficiently for him to start rubbing against it, very gently, the cord round his wrists.

"Mrs. Hakim, I am sorry for Nasib."

He sensed the alarm in her whisper. "You know his name?"

"I know. And the police know. He will not escape. It would be better for him if he did not commit any more crimes."

Then he realized that the old woman was no longer there. He could faintly hear her shuffle as she moved off along the hallway.

But by that time he was not concerned. He had felt the first strand of the cord fray and give. He started work on a second strand. The piece of glass came away from the crack and fell to the floor.

Muttering a curse, he groped for another piece, spent several long minutes wedging it, then gingerly tested it against the cord. A second strand parted, then a third. His hands eased apart. He could free first one, then the other, then hastily unknot the lashing round his ankles.

There was a stout hook on the back of the cupboard door, and a row of hooks on the side wall. Using some of the cord, he fastened the door hook to the others as securely as he could. That would give him a short respite if the door was pulled from the hallway.

There was no box in the cupboard, nothing upon which to clamber. But it was narrow enough for him to raise himself, by pressing against opposite walls, until he could reach the small window. Unlatched, it opened inwards. The frame was only sufficiently wide for him to get his head through, then to wedge his shoulders.

The window was in the side wall of a back addition to the house. To each pair of the terrace houses there was a similar back addition, containing the built-out kitchens on each floor.

Downwards from his window the wall dropped some forty feet into a basement yard; upwards it rose at least ten feet to a projecting flat roof on which stood the cold-water tank for the whole house. No possibility of escape either up or down.

He looked across the intervening space to the back addition to the next house. The kitchen immediately opposite suddenly lit up. A young woman came into sight in the sash window, to pile crockery into the kitchen sink.

Her window was slightly ajar at the top. She ought to be able to hear him if he called.

He tried. She made no response. He called more loudly. The woman raised her head, saw him, looked annoyed and pulled a curtain across the window.

In desperation Henry worked himself back into the cupboard and searched the shelf. On it stood a pile of plates. He took one, and managed to get the hand holding the plate, and that arm, his head and half his body squeezed through the window. With the other hand he held on to the inside of the window frame, steadying himself.

Then, with a muttered prayer for accuracy, he flung the

plate. It broke through the upper pane of the opposite kitchen window.

The curtain was pulled sharply back. The woman raised the lower window and leaned out. "What the hell . . . ?" she cried angrily.

He put his hand to his lips for quietness.

"Listen. There are Arab terrorists in this flat. I'm caught here and can't get out. Will you please phone Scotland Yard. Ask for Chief Inspector Comfort or Sergeant Chin. Give them the location of the flat—the second floor, but I don't know the number of the house. You will know that. Tell them it's Henry Theobald—that's me. Tell them to come quickly, and to come armed."

The woman was looking doubtful; probably wondering if he were mad.

"Please, please," he pleaded. "It can't be wrong to call the police. I'm not a lunatic. It's very serious. Make the phone call. Please. What can you lose?"

She stared at him for a moment, then raised a thumb in assent and moved out of sight. Henry waited. After several minutes, eternal minutes, the woman appeared again in the window opposite.

"Okay," she called. "They're coming."

He waved his thanks and pulled himself with difficulty back through the window. Then all he could do was wait. He looked at his watch. They could scarcely be here in less than ten minutes. A roving police car could get here sooner, but those men would not be armed.

He waited. Ten minutes passed. Nothing. Fifteen minutes. Nothing. Then the distant wail of a police-car siren, approaching. Then another.

It must be, he thought. It couldn't be cars on some other errand, coincidence.

But the sirens neared, then cut. A couple of minutes later there was hammering on the flat door, a shout for police entrance.

He heard the man running back through the hallway. He saw the cupboard door tugged. The cord between the hooks was holding. Henry grabbed at the door hook and clung on grimly. Otherwise he'd be a hostage.

The tugging strengthened. Henry could not get a firm grip on the hook in the door, and the hook in the wall was loosening. It could not hold much longer.

He felt for a piece of broken glass to defend himself when it gave. A piece of broken glass, he thought desperately, against a steel knife.

But then came the crash of the flat door breaking open. Henry heard the struggle in the hallway. It did not last long. Henry pulled the corded hook out of the wall. The cupboard door was jerked open, and there stood Sergeant Chin.

"So it really was you, sir," he exclaimed, almost unbelieving.

Henry pushed past him to find Comfort confronting the old woman. The man, handcuffed to a constable, was being led off.

"It's Mrs. Hakim," Henry told the detective. "She would have helped me if she could, but she was powerless. Nasib, her grandson, has gone somewhere to get instructions from his boss. She calls him mister. Where has Nasib gone, Mrs. Hakim? It's best now to help the police. Tell me, where has he gone?"

The old woman was weeping despairingly. "I not know, Mr. Theobald. I tell you, but I not know."

Comfort motioned to take her into one of the rooms.

"There's a policewoman coming to look after her. Now then, sir, how did you get here? What happened?"

Henry told him. Comfort's only comment was a grunt of appreciation. Henry asked if he could come to the Yard later to make a formal statement. He wanted to get back to Kate to let her know he was all right before she heard anything from the newspaper's crime man about the Earls Court raid.

"She's all right," he assured Comfort. "The office have laid on a staff car to take her wherever she goes, and the driver's an old friend, and a tough who can handle most situations. I expect she may be home by this time anyway."

"Of course make the statement later. There's one of my cars going in the King's Road direction. It'll drop you off at your flat if you like."

Kate was not in the flat. Henry poured himself a very large Scotch and swallowed it neat before he did anything else. Then, feeling better, he dialled the *Post* number and asked for Kate. She wasn't in the office, the switchboard told him, and put him through to the news desk.

"Hallo, Butch. Where's Kate?"

"Home. She sprained her ankle on the stairs here, so

Sam took her to the doctor, and then home. It's all right. Nothing broken, only a sprain. Just as well really, Henry. It'll keep her out of the way for a few days."

"But she isn't here."

"You're in the flat, and she's not there? Hell."

"Have you been in touch with her since you sent her home?"

"I phoned her a couple of times during the afternoon. Oh, and there was a chap came to the office wanting to talk to her. I wouldn't give him your number, of course, but I got the switch to call Kate and ask if she wanted to talk to him. She said she did, and he was put through." Butch asked someone there, probably his secretary, "What was the chap's name? Oh yes. Henry, his name was Sharp. Fred Sharp."

"Do you know what he told her?"

"Afraid not. He went into one of the booths."

"How long ago?"

"Not long. Quarter of an hour ago, maybe, perhaps a little longer."

"Call you back later," said Henry.

CHAPTER 17

When the office switchboard had told Kate that a Mr. Fred Sharp wanted to talk to her, she said yes, put him on.

"Something to tell me, Mr. Sharp?"

"Thought as you might want to know, missus. Thought perhaps you could find out, like."

"Find out about what?"

"Noises."

"Now come on, Mr. Sharp. Don't be mysterious, the way you were about that private detective. If you've something to tell me, tell me plainly, or I'll hang up."

"Noises in the house, missus. Two nights running, same time nearly. Round six o'clock."

"What sort of noises?"

"Footsteps."

Kate realized at once what that implied. There was a key to the shunt lock—one of the keys Cornelius had made on the portable cutter in the coins room where Miles lay dead. Whoever had got that key from Cornelius—and she could not guess who, or how—could get into the house. He could not switch off the perimeter alarm, even if he had Cornelius's key to the control panel, because the police had locked the cupboard itself. But the shunt-lock key alone would give admittance to the hall of the house, and to the coins room. The door to that room was the only door in the house not connected to the perimeter alarm. It was the master door to the valuables circuit, which was not in operation because the police had not thought it necessary to break open the wall safe that housed its controls, reckoning the perimeter alarm would suffice until the house was cleared of its contents.

"Sure it isn't the police?" she asked Sharp. "They've got Mr. Cabral's keys."

"Not them, missus. They've come several times, but they rings me up first in my basement. So I knows."

"Do you think whoever's there will be there tonight?"

"Couldn't say. But maybe. They were there the last two nights, about six o'clock. So I reckoned I'd tell you, and you'd find out through your newspaper. It weren't suicide, that I'll swear."

Kate looked at her watch. Ten minutes before six.

"Go straight back to your basement," she told Fred Sharp. "I'll meet you there. Then we can both listen if there's anything going on upstairs."

"Suppose there is. What do we do?"

"We cross bridges, Mr. Sharp, when we come to them."

Getting downstairs was more painful this time. Kate thought that her ankle must have swollen because she had used the foot too much, and there was considerable pressure from the binding. But she managed it, and the few steps along to King's Road, with the help of Henry's walking stick. She had luck with a taxi and was outside Cabral's house a few minutes after six.

Fred Sharp could not have got there as yet from the *Post* building, but he should not be long. It was not raining, though the evening was dark and cold. So she paid the taxi off. She would wait.

As on that evening when she had first arrived at the house with Henry, the street was deserted; only an empty car parked a few yards further on. Behind the windows of some of the houses were lighted rooms, but the single street lamp had failed altogether.

She looked up at the house. No light was showing anywhere. She began to wonder if there were anything at all in Fred Sharp's message. Suppose he wanted to get her there because . . . ? But she put that thought aside. He would certainly not, if that were his motive, have approached her openly through the office.

She went to the railing above the basement area and looked down. No light there either. Blackness.

As she was about to step back, a hand closed harshly on her mouth, the arm pressing on her throat.

"No noise," said a voice behind her. "Any noise, and this."

She felt the sharp point of a knife piercing her thick overcoat, actually pricking into the skin of her side. She nearly screamed, but just controlled herself. She hit out with Henry's walking stick, but it was knocked from her grasp.

"No noise," the voice repeated urgently.

She could feel the point of the knife again.

Now she was jerked away from the area railings, thrust up the two steps to the door of the house. Pain shot fiercely through her ankle. It was all she could do not to yell; but the knife point was still there.

Whoever held her was rapping on the door, a sort of code it seemed. She heard a key turn in a lock. The door opened. She was pushed inside.

The hall was in complete blackness. The man with the knife now held her by the body, and the knife point was touching her throat.

The front door quietly closed. One lock clicked home. The night latch. There was the sound of a key closing a second lock. The shunt lock.

The hall light flicked on, dazzling her eyes. Then she saw a man standing opposite her, a small revolver in his hand pointing at her.

A thin grey man.

After a tense moment she recognized him. That coin dealer, Harvey Foskett.

He regarded her sadly, grimly. "You were warned, Mrs. Theobald. Mrs. Hakim warned you. Nasib knocked you down in that alley and you must have known it was a warning. But you have been persistent. Foolishly persistent."

The man who was holding her was trying to interrupt.

"Yes, what is it, Nasib?"

"Her man is at the apartment, mister. We tied him up and Michel guards him."

Foskett frowned and stepped towards Kate. "How did your husband know where to go?"

She was aghast, bewildered. She might, she feared, faint. But she must not.

"Know how to go where? I don't know what you're talking about. Where is Henry?"

He stared at her hard for a minute, then seemed to accept that she did not know. He stepped back a few paces, murmuring, "It is unfortunate."

Suddenly Kate understood, "You killed Miles Cabral."

"Oh yes." He spoke of it calmly, as though relating some feat he had achieved. "He cheated me. You know about our operation with coins. You wrote about it in your newspaper. He was the principal. Miles bought the coins, and had the counterfeits made. I marketed them. For years, Mrs. Theobald. We had this arrangement for years."

He was telling her as though it were an interesting account of something harmless. Why was he telling her? Kate suddenly chilled as she listened.

Foskett went on, "He would never tell me who was making the counterfeits. He would never tell the forger how they were marketed. Thus Miles kept control. I thought my commission generous. Twenty per cent of his net proceeds—the sums for which I sold the coins, less what he had paid for the counterfeits. For years I was satisfied. I was a fool, a dupe."

Foskett smiled coldly. A smile looked grotesquely out of place.

"I guessed the work was being done in Beirut. Out of curiosity, simply curiosity, I made a journey there and at last, by various means, found Fouad Hakim. And then I discovered that Miles was cheating me. Had been cheating me, year after year, for many years. Cabral had been paying Fouad only half what he told me he had paid."

His gaze now was reminiscent, bitter, as though he were explaining to himself, reliving the anger of that discovery.

"So Fouad and I agreed," he said, suddenly smoother, calmer, "that it would be better if we worked together, without Miles. We would each have a half share. With my standing among the wealthiest collectors in the world, we would make millions instead of only thousands."

He was boasting now, showing off, Kate thought. It was as if he had been longing to display his cleverness and this was his opportunity.

"Fouad and I realized that Miles would have to be, shall we say, removed. I worked out a plan, and Fouad made a small machine that the plan entailed."

"A portable machine to cut keys."

"You are a brilliant young woman. What a pity . . ."

"How did Cornelius Ball come into it?"

She had a faint sort of hope that if only she could keep him talking, let him go on bragging . . . What she could hope for she did not know. And yet she felt some sort of hope, as he continued talking to her.

"Mr. Ball, like you, was too inquisitive. He was suspicious. I made a mistake in arranging for him to buy a copy of that penny. I should have remembered his connections with the Middle East. So he found Fouad. He came to know too much. Fouad sent me a message. If Mr. Ball eventually found his way to me, our whole future would dissolve into nothing. So Fouad sent his son to London, as my assistant. For Fouad and I both knew that Mr. Ball, also, must be removed."

He was looking grim again now. Hastily Kate tried to set him talking again.

"After you shot Miles Cabral, you simply set the alarm panel, then went out and locked the shunt lock from the outside of the front door?"

He nodded. "It was so simple," he said, with a self-satisfied smile. "The cleverest schemes are always simple."

But he seemed to be losing interest. He glanced back at the open door of the coins room, as though there were something he wanted to get on with.

Desperately Kate said, "So it was you who took those three coins."

"Not so. Miles had already taken them to Fouad in Beirut. Fouad still has them." He turned his cold smile on Nasib. "Your father thinks he can persuade me to grant him a larger share by surrendering those originals."

"You can't get away with it," Kate muttered, trying to convince herself.

"Why not, Mrs. Theobald? Miles and I got away with it for many years. Now I intend to get away with it, as you rather crudely put it. Nobody suspects Miles's death of being anything but self-inflicted—nobody, that is, except you and your husband. I do not propose to allow you and him to stand in my way, shall we say? I regret it. I regret it very much. But after all, what alternative have I?"

He glanced back again at the coins room. There must be some way of keeping him talking, of postponement. She could not conjure up any reason for hoping that it would help to postpone. But she somehow hoped . . .

"Was it on the pretext of delivering that Charles I crown that you came to this house that evening?"

"You are perceptive, Mrs. Theobald. Yes, of course that was my excuse. Cabral admitted me, of course. Why should he not? We went into the coins room, where I knew he kept his revolver. So I held him up with mine and shot him with his own. I should have taken at that time several other coins I particularly wanted, to continue our operations. But I was, perhaps, a little disconcerted. I had never before shot anybody. And then I had to concentrate on the manipulation with the keys. Replacing the originals in Miles's pocket as he lay there took more out of me than I had thought it would. I had, I found, less self-control than I usually demand of myself. So I left without the coins, and for three nights I have had to come back to choose those I want, from cabinets which my old friend Arthur Toogood has finished valuing.

"Now I have one or two more prime specimens to identify, then I shall not need to return and I can destroy the keys I cut.

"After I have located those coins, Mrs. Theobald, we must go. Until then, Nasib will keep an eye on you. Please do not try to outwit him, he is much too ready with that knife of his."

He turned and entered the coins room, switching on the light.

That was the moment when, at last, Kate fainted. Everything went fuzzy and she felt herself keeling over on to the carpet.

Directly Henry stopped talking to Butch he swaddled himself into his coat and ran down the stairs and towards the King's Road, calling a passing taxi.

Arriving at Cabral's house, he saw with relief that there was a light in the window of Fred Sharp's quarters in the basement. He stepped towards the area steps and kicked against something. He stooped to pick it up—his silver-knobbed walking stick.

Now he went swiftly down the steps and rang Sharp's doorbell. Sharp opened it at once. "Hallo, Mr. Theobald. I weren't expecting you."

"Where is my wife?"

"Couldn't say, guv. I went to that newspaper place to find her, on account of noises up there. They put me through on her phone, and she said to come here and she'd join me. But she ain't come. I been waiting."

Henry held out the walking stick.

"She has come. She had sprained her ankle and she must have taken this stick to walk with. It is my stick. It was lying in the roadway up there."

Sharp gaped at it.

"Blimey. There's noises again this evening, guv. Could they have got her?"

"Could who have got her?" demanded Henry, his stomach contracting with fear.

"Dunno. But the noises was on a few minutes ago."

Henry looked up. "In the house?"

Sharp said, "Wait a minute, guv."

He went back into his flat, and returned carrying an iron bar, his jemmy.

"I still got keys to the garage doors. Nobody asked for them. I can jemmy the door from the garage into the house, easy. You game to rush them?"

Henry gripped his arm. "Of course."

They stepped noiselessly up the steps, along the pavement past the front door of the house, to the garage. Sharp unlocked one of the garage doors and slid inside, for the first time lighting a small electric torch. Henry followed him past the Rolls to the door at the rear leading into the house.

Sharp handed him the torch. "Hold that, guv."

With unlikely delicacy he inserted the prong of the jemmy into the front edge of the door. Gently he eased it. It gave slightly. Then closed again.

Sharp stood back. "Give it a moment, guv. When we get it open, anyone inside'll hear it. Got to be quick then, eh? You got anything to muck about with? Wait a jiff."

He opened the boot of the car and handed Henry a heavy wrench. "It's a bit short, guv. You'll have to get close up, like."

Henry slipped the wrench up his sleeve, holding the end in his palm.

Sharp went back to the door, inserted the jemmy, suddenly put on pressure and the door swung right open with a loud crack.

Henry pushed him aside and raced in.

Kate was slumped in a chair, only half conscious, with Nasib Hakim standing beside her, his knife in his hand.

As Henry ran up the hall, a man came out of the lighted doorway of the coins room with a revolver in his hand.

"Just stand quite still where you are, Mr. Theobald."

"Foskett," cried Henry in astonishment.

He made to spring, but the gun did not waver. He saw Nasib poise the knife at Kate's throat. He stopped. Sharp, he realized, had not followed him in.

For a moment they all stood motionless, like a film suddenly halted on a screen.

Then Foskett spoke.

"We are leaving now. My car is parked a few yards away. Nasib will go first with your wife. Then you, Mr. Theobald. I will be behind you. If you make a noise, or any attempt to attract attention, or to run, it is not you who will suffer, but your wife. Nasib is expert with that knife."

Nasib pulled Kate up and pushed her towards the front door, the knife at her back.

Foskett stooped down to unlock the door, then motioned to Henry.

"Now you, Mr. Theobald."

Before Henry could move, there was a loud knocking on the door. Foskett jerked back. Nasib looked towards him uncertainly; what to do?

That was the unguarded moment when Henry slipped the wrench from his sleeve and caught Nasib behind the ear. The knife fell. As the man swung round, Henry hit him again. He dropped.

The knocking on the door resumed. From outside there was now a shout. "Police."

For one wild moment Henry thought Foskett would turn his revolver on Kate. But then two police constables came running up the hall from the door to the garage, Fred Sharp behind them.

Foskett stepped towards Kate as though to take a hostage. But he was too late. The constables were almost on him.

He swivelled the revolver to his temple and fired.

Henry took Kate in his arms, pressing her face to his shoulder, hiding the scene. "It's all right now, Kate. It's all right now."

Still half dazed, she mumbled, "What happened? The police . . ."

Henry smiled. "The famous burglar alarm. Fred triggered it with his jemmy."

A constable coming in from a parked police car reported that Detective Chief Inspector Comfort was on his way from Scotland Yard.

He was there within a few minutes.

"Kate has had a terrible time," said Henry. "I want to

take her home. I'll bring her to the Yard tomorrow, and by then she'll have recovered enough to tell you."

Comfort nodded. "Should she go to hospital?"

"Certainly not," interrupted Kate, coming round.

"She'll be all right," said Henry, "when she has had a good night's rest. I'll come back as soon as I can."

"Very good, sir."

The police operations men were coming in now, the photographers, the fingerprint men, the doctor. Nasib was being held by a couple of constables. He was spitting defiance. Comfort had turned away; so much to do.

Henry took Kate outside. They walked the few yards to the wider street and soon got a cruising taxi. He gave the driver their home address. Kate at once leaned forward and countermanded: "*Daily Post* building."

All she would answer to Henry's protests was, "Do shut up. I can catch the first edition."

So Henry kept quiet. But there was one thought nagging in his mind. The original 1954 penny—where was it?

At last he ventured, "It's obvious, isn't it, that it was Foskett who killed Cabral?"

Kate nodded.

"And so Foskett was part of the counterfeit operation?" Another nod.

He could hold it in no longer. "Darling, do you have any idea what happened to the 1954 penny?"

"Cabral took it to Fouad Hakim, with the two other coins from Rosemary's collection. Hakim still has them. Foskett said so."

"Legally," he murmured, "they belong to the Mint. Rosemary's uncle stole them. Could be a chance that the Government could get them back from Lebanon."

"I asked Geoff Wilton to follow up with Hakim. He may have been able to find out about the coins."

Butch was waiting at the office.

"Leave me be," she told Butch, "until I've written my piece. Yes, of course I'm all right."

She limped on Henry's walking stick to her desk, pulling across her typewriter.

A copy boy came over. "Message for you, Miss Theobald, from Beirut."

It was a service message from Geoff Wilton: "Hakim killed in shellfire last night. Workshop and all contents destroyed."